Meet the For

JACK SWAYNE

The leader of the team. A brilliant tactician and superb soldier. For him, failure is not an option . . . ever.

"PERFECT"

The new guy—with a mind so razor sharp he does crossword puzzles *without* the clues. But can he live up to his name under fire?

NIGHT RUNNER

A full-blooded American Indian. Even with the cutting-edge technology used by the team, the deadliest thing about him is his senses.

FRIEL

An ex–street thug turned disciplined Marine. A natural-born killer with no remorse. Possibly the deadliest shot in the world.

FORCE RECON

The explosive new series by
James V. Smith, Jr.

FORCE RECON

THE BUTCHER'S BILL

James V. Smith, Jr.

BERKLEY BOOKS, NEW YORK

This is a work of fiction. Names, characters, places, and incidents either are the product of the author's imagination or are used fictitiously, and any resemblance to actual persons, living or dead, business establishments, events, or locales is entirely coincidental.

FORCE RECON: THE BUTCHER'S BILL

A Berkley Book / published by arrangement with the author

PRINTING HISTORY
Berkley edition / October 2001

All rights reserved.
Copyright © 2001 by James V. Smith, Jr.

This book, or parts thereof, may not be reproduced in any form without permission.
For information address: The Berkley Publishing Group,
a division of Penguin Putnam Inc.,
375 Hudson Street, New York, New York 10014.

Visit our website at
www.penguinputnam.com

ISBN: 0-425-17814-5

BERKLEY®
Berkley Books are published by The Berkley Publishing Group,
a division of Penguin Putnam Inc.,
375 Hudson Street, New York, New York 10014.
BERKLEY and the "B" design
are trademarks belonging to Penguin Putnam Inc.

PRINTED IN THE UNITED STATES OF AMERICA

10 9 8 7 6 5 4 3 2 1

For all the victims

Event Scenario 16—Day 1

"Ambush."

One word. A practiced signal.

So the members of Force Recon Team 2400, Team Midnight, reacted as they had practiced dozens of times, with instant, deadly urgency at what was spoken into their earphones.

Night Runner, walking point, dropped to his knees and rolled off the trail. Without a pause, he came up in a low crouch and slunk off. Without a sound, he cleared the area so no enemy could open fire at the last spot where he had stood and catch him with a lucky shot. Without a doubt, it looked as if he'd simply evaporated into the night.

After he had crept twenty meters away in a zigzag pattern, he put everything in his high-tech arsenal to work at locating the danger reported in that one-word signal. First his thermal-imaging nightscope. Then an experimental electronic ear that had proven able to hear a man's breathing at a hundred meters. Most importantly, the physical senses of a Blackfeet warrior. Eyes, ears, and nose—detection devices that had been honed on the last mission into Iraq. And in the months since, in a self-imposed regimen of fasting, sweating, exercise, and prayer to the deities of his people. That and a regimen of ice. A regimen more demanding than any Marine training course.

Any.

Including Force Recon. A regimen, he vowed, he would honor the rest of his life. A regimen that would never let him go soft again, as he had before Iraq, their last outing.

He had literally punished himself according to the custom of the true Blackfeet brave. A torturous workout that would have killed anything less than a Blackfeet warrior Force Recon Marine.

FRIEL DROPPED TO a crouch and rolled to his right, off the trail. He came up on one knee, the latest version of his experimental smart gun sweeping the woods for a target. He scanned 360 degrees as fast as he could turn without making noise. The scope on the 20-mm rifle took in everything in its path, a fan of twenty degrees with sensors to pick up thermal images, magnetic impulses, and radar returns, along with the newest item in the gadget inventory, a digital imager that would compare and contrast every item in the electronic screen.

Friel did not try to look at the images streaking across his screen, did not pause to decipher them, interpret them. The digital sensors worked faster than his own senses, so he let them carry the freight.

Friel's gun picked up five hits. Hits that showed up as green in the preprogrammed inventory scale, which he had dubbed the piss scale. Nothing came up red in the target inventory scale. So Friel lifted his rifle and scanned the treetops. Still nothing.

He pointed the weapon at the new guy on the team. Image No. 3, "FNG" on the piss scale, began to blink. Private First Class Gordon I., for Irving, Perfect. In the pre-mission setup of his sniper gun's computer, Friel had had so many choices of IDs. Gordo. Gip. The Gipper. Mr. Perfect. Dumbshit. He chose FNG, for Freaking New Guy.

The scope showed FNG to be one of the targets that had been imaged from every angle before the mission so the rifle's computer could identify him in a combat situation and paint him green on the screen. Eliminate him as a threat. Save him from being a victim of friendly fire. Friel caressed his trigger.

"Freaking New Guy," he muttered to himself. What he wouldn't give for a blinking red indicator in the target inventory scale right now. A little battlefield accident might be just the thing to cheer him up. *Screw the new guy and the dog he rode in on.* Except that such an accident would be hard to explain. The gun would not fire at Perfect unless Friel touched an override button near the trigger guard. The onboard image would be saved in the gun computer's memory like one of those black boxes on airliners.

A board of inquiry would look into the killing of the Marine, would see that he'd been intentionally shot.

Friel shook his head. *Damn shame.*

PERFECT REACTED AS he'd been taught, rolling off the path in the opposite direction from the man in front of him. He crawled on his belly for ten meters to the base of a tree, its bark rough and gullied. Then he rose up on one knee. Planting his left shoulder into a crevasse in the bark, he scanned the range fan available to him.

First he found Gus in the night-vision scope. Gus, the perfect soldier, was doing what he was supposed to be doing. Of course. Of course the dog had slunk away from the trail—perfectly trained. Of course Gus now slithered by him to observe with his nose and eyes the terrain on the other side of the tree. Again, perfectly trained. Even Perfect's supervising trainers in the dog course had marveled at this little trick. How did the dog know to watch his handler's six?

Morons. Instead of hand signals, you just train the animal to watch the muzzle of your rifle. Only don't train the dog to look in the direction the gun pointed. That was a human tendency. Teach the animal to recon the opposite direction.

Go against the tendencies, always look for the misdirection. The magician flutters one hand? Avoid the flourish. Catch him slipping the dollar into his pocket with the other hand. The boss rubs his chin? Look for him to be scratching his balls at the same time. The enemy comes at you with a noisy demonstration from the south? Better be ready for the sneak attack from the north. Or more likely the east or west.

Perfect knew all the cons. He'd used all the good ones himself.

The aiming point of his rifle fell on Friel. Speaking of cons. Friel was looking at him in his own scope. Friel. What a joke. A firecracker was what he was. All noise and no poise. He had Friel's number, knew that he was mostly talk, all flourish and flutter. Sure, he'd been in the action and killed a few bad guys. And sure, he hadn't disgraced himself. But he'd blown it big-time on his last mission. Nobody was talking about how the big guy, Potts, had been lost in action. Sure as hell, because nobody was telling the story, Perfect knew Perfectly well there was a story to tell. The misdirection thing. All the boys on his team kept their lips zipped. The Indian because he was the strong silent type. The captain because he was the captain by the book. Those two he'd never crack. But Friel? Any other day, any other subject, and he'd be shooting his mouth off all over town. Secrets or no secrets. High security or not. Friel was a talker, a braggart, the bullshitter of all bullshitters. Perfect knew the type.

Except Friel wasn't bragging about the last mission. Something had happened that was less than brag-able, even un-brag-able.

Friel was keeping his mouth shut because he was ashamed of something. Perfect understood shame, knew how to pry open the shamed. Like opening a can of sardines with a push-button lid. Push all the right buttons in the right order.

Perfect and Friel had locked onto each other with their deadly rifles in a kind of death stare.

Perfect blinked first. He shifted his scope away.

Let the Boston bad-ass think he was weaker. Button number one. And stupider. Just because he was from Indiana—a stupid Hoosier, that's what Friel thought. Button number two.

AT THE WORD *ambush,* Swayne whirled and dropped in a single motion, hooking the butt of his rifle behind the knees of the man at his shoulder. The knees buckled. Before the man could utter a sound, Swayne clapped a hand over his mouth and laid the blade of his bayonet alongside the hawk nose.

"Not a sound, you bastard." The tip of the bayonet covered the man's eyebrow. Swayne drew the blade backward an inch. Maybe the man could see the threat of its silhouette against the sky. Maybe not. Didn't matter. Swayne didn't intend for it to be a threat, but a promise. If the guy tried to call out, or if a single bullet was fired in the direction of the Force Recon Team, Swayne was going to give the Kosovar rebel a lobotomy. Right through the eye socket. A surgical procedure taught to him by Night Runner. One that, to his knowledge, nobody had yet survived.

The guy got the point. He didn't struggle. Didn't move. Hadn't yet even breathed, although he must have

been feeling more than a little pain from the rifle stock
still locked behind his knees as he lay bent over backward. He blinked a lot, though. Perhaps from the misting
raindrops falling in his eyes. Perhaps in sheer terror.

After a mere three seconds had passed, Swayne's anger at the Kosovar passed. He should have had a secondary report by now. Or else the ambush should have
been triggered. Or else Perfect had made a new-guy mistake in speaking the word *ambush*.

The Spartans' code was a simple one. A word beginning with the letter *A* meant imminent danger of enemy
contact, probably with a superior force. A one-word signal using the letter *B* told the team that an enemy force
was in sight but either it did not pose a radical threat,
or the team could handle the force. The letter *C* was a
routine sighting. The code had nothing to do with radio
security. Electronic scramblers took care of that. It simply allowed a team member to alert everybody and de-
scribe the general situation by using only one word.
When an enemy had eyes and ears near enough to see
and hear, special operations forces could not afford to
resort to lengthy radio chatter.

And a word like *ambush* meant a hell of a lot more
than something like *alligator,* which Night Runner had
used on the last mission, and it didn't require a Force
Recon Marine to figure it out.

Swayne put a hand over his boom mike. "Team, this
is Spartan One," he growled. "Report."

"THIS IS TWO," Night Runner said. He turned down the
volume in the earpiece plugged into his left ear. Not that
the captain had spoken so loudly. Just that his hearing
had grown so sensitive in the last months of his spartan
warrior training.

The forest had yielded nothing to any of Night Runner's senses. Not a hint. Even after he had changed po-

sition three more times. The new guy, who had given the signal, was wrong. The Gunny would have his ass for it, too, in the debrief—

There was no Gunny. No other Gunny, that is. He, Night Runner, was the Gunny now, newly promoted to fill the shoes of Gunnery Sergeant Delmont Potts, who had given his life to save Friel's on the last mission. Now it was up to him to have the man's ass. Dammit. He didn't want to be the chief. Why couldn't the Marine Corps just let him be an Indian?

"THREE, NEGATIVE," FRIEL reported. Sergeant Henry Friel now that he, too, had been promoted. If the boys in the hood could only see him now. A Marine Sergeant, for Ripley's freaking believe it or not. Here he was a real live buck sergeant. With the electronic bead of his 20-mm trained on the right eye of a subordinate Marine. Wishing for an opportunity to kill the man. *You talk about your cognitive dissonance—*

The red indicator blinked in Friel's scope. The gun's computer had finished processing what it had seen in Friel's sweep a few seconds ago. It had spotted something out of place after all. At the four o'clock position on the perimeter of the image area, head-high. Friel swung off the FNG's wide-open eyeball, no longer feeling homicidal toward the intruder who had taken over Gunny Potts's spot on the team. Now all business.

As he swung his gun through its arc, the spot on the perimeter of the scope flew toward the center of the image area. Friel could not pick up an identifiable target. So he pressed a button on the forestock of his rifle, asking the computer for help.

"Belay my last," Friel said. There was something out of place in the forest after all. Something besides the Force Recon Team that didn't belong in Kosovo, the country torn by civil war. The instant the computer put words on the screen of his scope, he repeated them aloud into the boom mike at his lips: "Horizontal metallic linear irregularity."

The words did not click with him. *What da freakin hell's at rat-bastid, cheese-eatin, ovah-educated freakin computeh tryinah say in two-dollah weds anyways? Couldn't the fo-wide Havvid pissants teach it to talk in suntin besides pig-freakin-Latin, oh wedevveh?*

He'd not met many scientists, but he'd run across a few who'd tried to teach him the ABC's of the various experimental weapons he would eventually carry in the field. As far as he was concerned, every one of them needed an enema. He'd like to go Preparation H on the Mooks that programmed the chip in his gun. Give them a burst of six right up the old—

Night Runner spoke in his headset. "Possible trip wire."

"Trip whya?" The instant Night Runner said it, Friel's eye could identify it in the scope. *Horizontal metallic linear irregularity? The bastid computeh couldn't just say trip whya?*

Even as he stewed, Friel changed his position, finding new cover as he retraced his steps ten meters or so. He set up so he could cover Night Runner when the captain gave the order to pull back. Oh, and the FNG and the dog he rode in on. Much as he didn't care about them two, he would have to protect their asses, too.

"Rally on One," came Swayne's command. "Offset niner times one."

Friel scanned the forest beyond the trip wire. His job was to cover the six of Night Runner and FNG as they pulled back to the position Swayne had given them. He couldn't spot Night Runner in his scope. Didn't expect to. The chief had ways of moving that broke all the laws of nature. Only the freakin' fog could get around the way he did, so Friel had long ago stopped being surprised when he couldn't find the man until he put a hand on his shoulder.

No such problem with the FNG. He stepped backward, away from the wire, and fell right on his ass. Friel snickered into his boom mike and uttered a curse word so the Brownie scout could know he'd been spotted doing butt-stomps in the forest.

NIGHT RUNNER WASTED no time getting on him. "Three, do you have a report?"

"That's a neg."

"Then knock it off. Clear the area. Both of you. On the double." Night Runner watched Friel cast about with his experimental scope, trying to pick him up. He smiled to himself. High-tech or no, Friel wasn't about to see him, because Night Runner had already moved behind him, less than ten meters away. He had seen Perfect fall on his butt, too. The kid was clumsy but composed. He had held his breath and didn't make a sound. And he had kept his weapons and gear from clattering. Next, the kid moved off the trail and paused to calculate the position where he was to rally. Using his handheld computer with global positioning screen, he would identify Swayne's Personal Locator Beacon. The PERLOBE return, uplinked to a satellite and downlinked to him, would blink until Swayne actually arrived at the spot.

Perfect moved from spot to spot and kept trying to set his PERLOBE. The instrument was having its troubles on this mission. The mountains and forest seemed to be having effects that Night Runner hadn't seen before. Maybe it was simple line-of-sight problems. Or maybe magnetic interferences in the atmosphere or in the earth. Or even operator malfunction. Runner was glad he didn't have to rely so much on machines and electronics. He had himself, his warrior heritage, his Marine training. And a sense of direction so infallible it sometimes surprised even him.

Finally Perfect set his course and moved out carefully, pointing the way with a hand signal for his dog, a golden retriever specially trained for this mission. The dog took up the heading pointed out to him. Gus stalked his way through the forest, more a cat than a dog, traveling as he had been trained, without a sound.

PERFECT HAD TO laugh. The thing about falling over on his ass when he got the word to move out. He'd dreamed that up on the spot. Pure genius, too. Make the Boston bozo think he was clumsy, too. Button number three.

NIGHT RUNNER SAW that the kid from Indianapolis had taken up the right heading. He was pleased at Perfect's progress. He wanted to like the kid. Wanted to give him a chance. It was just that something about him never clicked into place the way it should. He'd never failed at a training exercise. In fact, he'd always come up with inventive solutions to problems thrown at him.

Trouble was, Perfect would take an off-the-wall path even when a straight line was the best solution. Even in situations that had nothing to do with the tactical.

Runner thought about it a second. Yeah, the kid would go out of his way to go out of his way. Images flashed at him. Quantico was just one of the many bases where Force Recon maintained a secret training compound. One exercise was a maze where teams would have to send men in one at a time to see how they tackled physical obstacles with abstract dimensions. When they turned Perfect loose in the anteroom of the maze, he ran outside, found the exit, and worked the puzzle backward. In record time, too. The umpires wanted to disqualify him. Runner wouldn't have it. None of the rules said a Marine had to solve the maze from beginning to end. Nothing seemed unfair in taking it from end to start. Even if Perfect's time eclipsed the previous record. Set by one Sergeant Robert Night Runner.

Then again, Perfect even ate funny, now that Runner thought about it. You hand a normal person a kiwi fruit and they'll eat it one of several ways. They'll peel it like a boiled egg. Or cut it into halves and scoop out the meat with a spoon. Or cut it into wedges like an orange and scoop it out with their front teeth.

Not Perfect. He put it into his mouth whole. Chewed it like a peeled Easter egg. And spat out the furry husk.

Runner shook his head. For the sake of Granny's apple butter, he thought, using one of Potts's exclamations.

That was it! Perfect did *everything* differently. He ate fried chicken with a fork and knife, but picked up a steak with his fingers. Didn't wear socks or underwear. Brushed his teeth before and after meals. Ate his dessert first, then his meal, then his salad.

He used rubbing alcohol instead of after-shave. Runner smiled at that one. He did the same as the kid on that one. He did it because it would soothe his skin like after-shave lotion but not leave a scent that could betray him to an enemy like the Bedouin on the last mission.

Runner began to recall other situations where Perfect had pulled things like that. There were more. Once he had caught the kid working a crossword puzzle without clues. The kid had smiled up at him when he'd asked about it.

"Gunny," Perfect had said, his smile getting wide enough to be stupid. "It's no challenge to work a crossword puzzle the normal way. I cut the puzzle out of the paper and throw away the clues. Then I put my own words into the puzzle. If you want, I'll do one of mine and make up clues for you to work it."

The stupid smile. The kid playing at a game that required a modest genius. The two didn't add up. Night Runner understood. The kid had been dumbing down, trying to draw Night Runner into asking stupid questions. But Perfect wasn't dumb. He was clever. Too clever for Night Runner's liking. Smart as a weasel.

But it was time to move out. And this was no place

on earth to be playing mind solitaire, trying to figure out Perfect's psychosis.

Especially since Night Runner had missed the trip wire. Traveling in a stealthy crouch, bent low, legs bunched and ready to propel him off the trail. He'd walked right under the wire. Damn!

He gave himself the severest of reprimands for making a mistake that was so fundamental. Like the whitetail deer, who had no enemies from the sky and so never looked to the trees, he'd focused all his attention forward and to the sides. He'd watched his step too literally and too much.

Any lamebrained animal killer could walk up a rope ladder to a tree stand and, sitting in a lawn chair strapped to the tree trunk in plain sight, wait for the deer to walk into his line of fire. Any bozo could ambush the unwary animal.

He'd acted like a whitetail fawn. Still red and spotted and raw and dumb. Damn!

But enough of that. He had the mission to attend to. And his men. He should be watching for their mistakes, which would be so much more elementary than his own. So he watched the new guy.

Perfect followed the dog toward the rally point. The kid moved quietly for a city kid. And he was smart. He understood that it was better to follow the animal than try to divide his attention between sneaking through the woods and keeping an eye on his GPS. Gus would stay on course until somebody gave him a new direction. Perfect was almost perfect. Night Runner would have to coach him about only one thing—not striking off on a straight line toward a rally point or any other kind of destination. Better to move in an off-direction first. And close on the rally point from a random line. Don't let an enemy make any assumptions about what your destination might be. As Runner had done in Iraq.

Then he did a mental take. Perfect knew the rule. He

was breaking it on purpose. Just to be different? Runner would have to watch him more closely. Creative tactics were one thing. But the team couldn't afford a guy going against the grain just to be different. Not if it was going to risk the team.

He saw Friel shake his head in disgust at the new kid. Pretty funny that. Potts, Night Runner, and Captain had had to keep on Friel's tail on every one of his first four missions before he stopped traveling like the crow in flight to the nest.

When Perfect had moved out of sight, Friel used little more than a moment and three locations to reset his own GPS, then struck out in the opposite direction. Night Runner kept watch, both to provide security for his men and to grade their performance. Something he hadn't had to do in his previous life when he was just the team scout and No. 2 shooter behind Friel.

Night Runner needed a moment to think about how he could tighten up his new team. Friel wasn't exactly being trouble. He was just being Friel. But he should have accepted the new guy by now. Night Runner understood that nobody could come to this team after Potts's death and be accepted right away. He had known it would take time. But he had not expected that it would take so much time for Henry Friel. The loss of Potts in Iraq had changed Friel in ways that nobody on the team could understand, including Friel.

Night Runner wondered whether the man would have to be pulled from field duty for a while. Get a mental eval. Fitness-for-duty exam. Night Runner shook his head. He might not be suited to be the Gunny on this team, but he knew well enough that simply giving Friel a fitness-for-duty or mental or any other kind of exam would render him unfit. *Damn,* he hated this leadership role. Operating alone was how he operated best. Yes, he could adapt himself to take orders, especially from an officer like Swayne. But giving orders? *Damn!*

• • •

SWAYNE SHUT OFF the microphone with his knife hand, keeping the other over the mouth of Petr, his so-called guide. He put the tip of the bayonet back near the eyeball before he spoke.

"I'm going to take my hand off your mouth," he growled. "One sound, and you're a dead man. Understand my English?"

The head bobbed ever so slightly because the man was unwilling to poke himself on the tip of Swayne's combat dagger.

Swayne repositioned his hand to Petr's throat.

"My legs," the man hissed.

"Shut up. There's a wire up ahead. What do you know about that?"

"I know nothing," Petr said, his accent thick. "You must trust me. You must—"

Swayne slapped Petr's forehead with the flat of his bayonet blade to let him know the man wouldn't be dictating trust or any other musts to him. He rolled him over onto his face, removing his rifle from behind the man's knees. He touched the tip of his knife to the occipital area of the skull where head meets neck—not speaking a word but sending his threat in the form of a prick of pain. One arm at a time, he pulled the man's wrists behind him. One wrist at a time, he ratcheted a nylon tie-strap tight. Then he joined the two straps with a third, forming a set of field-expedient handcuffs.

Petr gasped.

"We are friends," he whined. "Our countries are allies against the Serbs. We—"

Swayne whacked him with the knife blade again. Then he reached into a jacket pocket and removed a packet that looked like an oversized Band-Aid. He took off the backing carefully and clapped a strip of tape over the man's mouth. Bad-ass duct tape, Friel called it, although it had very little in common with ordinary tape.

NASA had developed it for emergency repair kits in spacecraft after the near-disaster of Apollo 13. Its fabric was a class of compounds by itself, a combination of synthetic fabrics and metals, capable of withstanding extreme temperatures and tensions unmatched even by the material in a spider's web. Its adhesive would stick to anything except liquids or oils, and once applied, would not fail. During the Gulf War, maintenance crews had temporarily repaired one-inch holes in the skin of fighters that had been hit by stray flak. The tape had kept the aircraft flying at the supersonic speeds until more permanent repairs could be made. But crews found that the tape could not be removed except by cutting out entire patches of metal aircraft skin. So NASA had had to go back to work to develop two-step chemical solutions that could dissolve both the tape and its adhesive.

Naturally there had been accidents and pranks, fingers taped together and genitals taped shut. So the material had been banned except for supervised maintenance uses. And in special operations like Force Recon, where almost anything could be used as a weapon.

Swayne pulled Petr to his feet, checked his own digital wrist compass, plotted a three-legged course, and pointed in the direction he wanted the man to travel first. Petr's eyes glittered in the scant moonlight. He took two steps backward.

Swayne grabbed him by the shoulder and spun him, pushing him where the compass pointed. Petr, his eyeballs flashing like convex mirrors, turned to face him.

Swayne's first instinct was to lash out, but suddenly he understood. Kosovo was a land where atrocity had become as commonplace as nightfall, where decency had gone extinct. Petr had probably treated many a dearly departed Serb soldier exactly as Swayne was now treating him. Moments before putting a slug into the back of a Bosnian head.

Swayne decided to use the man's emotions as a truth

test. He stepped up and spoke down into his ear, enunciating every word. "I am an American Marine officer and an honorable man. I am not going to kill you." He saw the doubt in the man's eyes, but it was hopeful doubt. "Unless you have betrayed my team."

Petr reacted with a slight widening of his eyes and a tiny inhalation through his nose. Swayne couldn't be sure whether to read it as relief that he would not be killed after all, or as fear that he would.

Swayne would have to think about it, analyze it, perhaps talk it over with Night Runner. Maybe later they could decide how much to trust this guy. For now he had to get moving.

"I'm not afraid to look you in the eyes when I kill you," he growled into the man's face. "Right now I'm in a hurry to join the rest of my team. You're not going to cause me to be late, are you? Force me to leave you behind?"

Petr reacted immediately to the new threat. He shook his head.

Swayne pointed. Petr moved out.

They had not traveled ten meters before Petr fell. Hard.

No, he had thrown himself—

Swayne heard a screech.

He dove, rolled onto his face, and covered his ears with the palms of his hands. The explosion's ground wave hit them an instant before the sound. The earth thrust itself at Swayne, and he cringed, waiting for the secondary effects.

It didn't take long. First came the roar of sound and concussion slapping their way through the foliage. Around him, trees squealed as they rasped against other trees on the way to the forest floor. Then came the crashes of timber all around them, screams and cracks like gunshots of breaking branches, splitting trunks. Down came branches. Then twigs. Leaves and needles drifted down. The occasional tree trunk smashed against the ground as if some giant was thrashing the earth.

Relative silence followed. Forest animals chirped and squawked in protest at having their sleep disturbed. The team reported in turn that they had survived.

Swayne crawled to Petr and found him alive and trembling.

He murmured against the tape.

Swayne trembled, too. Not in fear but rage. Somebody was shooting heavy ordnance at them. But intentionally? The man had heard the sound before him, almost as if expecting it.

Then his reason caught up to him, and Swayne settled down. Of course the man from Kosovo had heard the screech of the rocket first. His life on the run from Serbs had conditioned him to react to the sound that must have come at him almost daily for months, if not years. Why wouldn't he dive at even the sigh of the sound?

Swayne had to chide himself for getting too upset. The object of an on-target artillery shell never heard a sound. Only the noise of missiles flying by or overheard, long past, made it to the ears of others.

From what he could tell, the round had hit in the vicinity of the wire. What did that mean? That was the question of greater importance. Did the Serbs have sensors? Was the wire a transmitter rather than a booby trap? Or had Petr led the team to the spot that had been a preplanned target, expecting to vanish into the forest and leave the Spartans to be hit?

A lot of questions. And answers, he had none. He should get collected, both as a team and in his head. Then put some questions to his boy Petr. Try to get to the bottom of coincidences he didn't like seeing.

Short of the rally point, Swayne surveyed the area with night-vision binoculars from fifty meters away across a clearing. He found that Friel and Perfect had already arrived and established security by putting their backs toward each other with ten meters between them, covering the east and west approaches at the margin of the forest. He saw that Perfect's dog formed the third point of a triangle, facing south, looking over a ridgeline. Gus lay on his belly, ears perked as if on guard. Swayne did not doubt the dog's sentry ability, although he had been trained for other, more grisly duties.

Swayne gave Petr a course change that would take them around the clearing. As the man stepped out in the new direction, Swayne kept his binoculars on the golden retriever.

The animal's head swiveled until it was looking directly at them. Then, crawling on its belly, it swapped ends, never taking its eyes off the Kosovar guide. Swayne checked Friel and Perfect. The dog had apparently given them some kind of signal, for both Marines had trained their weapons in his direction.

"This is One," Swayne murmured into his boom mike. "Two of us are now coming in from an angle to the direction you are now looking."

"Four, roger," said Perfect, sweeping the area with his own night-vision sight, apparently not yet finding Swayne and the Kosovar.

Friel grunted. Swayne watched as the sergeant's sniper gun swept past the Kosovar, then swung back to identify him, then came back toward Swayne, who ducked behind a tree and waved his binoculars.

"Do you have an ID on my NVGs?" Swayne asked.

Friel grunted, and only then did Swayne peek from behind the cover of the three-foot-thick tree. He had seen Friel's electronic marvel of a sniper gun in action during training sessions before this mission. To his mind, weapons were becoming far too clever. Too many circuits. Too many computer chips. Too many sensors. It all added up to one thing: too many things to go wrong. Digital target identification. Electronic firing. What happens if the tiny current of electricity crosses over from one circuit to the other? So that the gun no longer stops at identifying targets but takes the liberty of killing them as well?

Swayne saw Friel give him a thumbs-up signal and lift up the muzzle of his gun. So he stepped out from behind the tree and followed in the footsteps of his guide or captive or traitor or whatever in hell he was.

Forget about the gun and all its electronics, he told himself. Friel could be trusted even if the gun could not. Forget about Petr. Whether he trusted him or not, the man was entirely under his control, managed by a few strips of synthetic straps and bad-ass tape.

Time he put his mind to work on this mission. Time to calculate how to get on with it now that the trip wire had diverted them from their original course. This was to be, he knew, one of the toughest missions his team would undertake. Team 2400, called Team Midnight for the obvious reason, had always been better suited to combat than to strictly surveillance missions. Oh, his four-man unit could creep around with the best of them. They could remain undetected anywhere in the world. Ability was not the problem. Temperament. That was the rub. The chemistry of his men. They would rather shoot than spy. Rather kill than creep. But for this mission stealth was the keyword. They were to remain invisible. In and out of Kosovo, collecting information without leaving a sign of ever having been there.

A mission of global importance. That was what Swayne's boss had called it. Implications, not just for people and countries, but for humankind and civilization itself.

Swayne might have taken Colonel Zavello seriously. Except that every other word had been an obscenity. Zavello had apparently been given specific orders. And those orders had been passed to the Spartans verbatim— except for the curse words.

Swayne might have laughed. Except that Zavello had been seething, consuming himself in a fury of self-imposed discipline. Swayne knew that Zavello had been admonished by the National Security Adviser face-to-face after the last mission, after Zavello had played a game of cops-and-robbers with the White House. They had reined him in, threatened him with forced retirement, the absolute worst possible punishment. Zavello could not have survived a week. Wearing civilian clothes over the weekend alone was almost too much for him. But every day? And no combat missions to direct from long range? No living vicariously through Force Recon teams committed all over the world? There would be no living at all.

So Swayne had done the only thing he could do. He had saluted and left the briefing room as quickly as he could. Zavello might be a ballistic missile looking for a place to strike, but he could be avoided.

This mission was another matter.

The Spartans had to indict their enemy—an enemy not just of the team or the Marine Corps, but of humanity. They had to find evidence of atrocities. If possible, catch that enemy in action, committing the most heinous of crimes. Mass murders. Individual executions. Gang rapes. Torture. Crimes that might be cause for war, but crimes that the Force Recon Team could not react to with so much as a polite request to cease and desist. Swayne's team had no latitude in the matter. Their orders had come from the National Command Authority. The President. Verbatim—almost.

Swayne had sworn to obey any such orders, even when they did not come from the President himself but from one of the many thousands of officers who were superior to Swayne in rank. This time, though, the orders came from the man himself, through Zavello, to Swayne.

And his dilemma now and from the very moment

when he had been given the orders was that he had no intention of obeying them.

Instead of using his almost psychic ability to foresee glitches in tactics and changes in battle, and to select any number of courses of action to counter those changes, Swayne found himself behaving like an amateur. He found himself hoping that he would fail to find his enemy. And if he should encounter him by accident, he wished that the enemy would choose not to commit the crime that the Force Recon Team had been sent out to witness. And if that enemy were to commit that crime in Swayne's sight, that Swayne and his team would do what they had been sent to do: transmit live video and vanish.

Knowing all the while that the Spartans would find the enemy and record the crime. Even as they did whatever they could to intervene and prevent it.

PRISTINA, KOSOVO—0107 LOCAL

"CRIMES AGAINST HUMANITY," said Nina Chase, almost-but-not-quite-ace foreign correspondent for CNN. "You know exactly what I'm talking about, General Markocevik. The concentration camps. Extermination of ethnic groups. Death squads. Mass executions. You know what I mean. Crimes against humanity."

"Of course, of course," said Markocevik. He smiled broadly, warmly. "Always the crimes against humanity. This is what we are accused of, which is what every breakaway republic always accuses its mother country of committing, wouldn't you say? Isn't that what your original thirteen colonies said about Mother England?" He shrugged. "In your Declaration of Independence?"

Nina watched him lift a glass of unusual white wine to his lips. Unusual because it had come to her warm—

not just room temperature, but lukewarm, as if it had been heated.

At her first drink, she'd wrinkled her nose and nearly spat it back into the glass.

"You expected it to be cold," he'd said matter-of-factly. "I should have warned you."

When she'd drunk it as he had instructed her, sipping it as if it were hot tea, a bouquet of fruit had exploded in her mouth. The combination of flavor and sipping had given the illusion that the wine was chilled.

"My God," she'd said. "That's the most extraordinary drink I've ever tasted."

"Thank you."

"You call this wine?"

"Yes, I do. And thank you again."

"For what?"

"For calling it wine. Actually, it's an extremely light liqueur, but I'm trying to market it as a table wine. To appeal to you Americans." He'd lifted his glass toward hers. "After this—rebellion unpleasantness is dispensed with, and we have established normal relations."

He began a diatribe about his plans for breaking into the international liquor market. She studied him, paying no attention to the liquor lecture. He was handsome, maybe the most handsome man she'd ever known next to Jack Swayne. She felt guilty for a moment, always leaving Jack behind. Now she was sitting in this intimate corner of a hotel bar. A hotel, incidentally, owned by Markocevik. When he smiled, he hit the high beams, as if to show off every one of his porcelain caps, each as white as a urinal. Now and then he would pause to take a drink, and his teeth would flash blue like static electricity through the fishbowl of his glass. He'd suggested that she sip her wine, but he drank his in long drafts.

He had a tan, obviously artificial, because in the four weeks she had been in this country she had not seen the sun on more than four days. For less than an hour each time, and just before sunset at that.

He was forty-six years old, according to his bio, but his hair coloring, black and shiny as a pay phone, gave him back more than half a dozen years. Beneath the exquisite tailoring of his tuxedo, she could see the fitness that could have come only from nonstop mission training like Jack Swayne's. Or from well-spent hours in the gym, working out on the machines.

He had finished talking. For how long, she did not know. Had he asked her a question? She did not know that either, and hadn't a clue about what kind of an answer to fake if he had. He stared at her, a glittering smile playing at the corners of his mouth.

But no longer a friendly smile. And in his eyes she saw anything but warmth. They radiated the cold like reverse microwaves, chilling rather than heating. She knew the look of a murderer. She had seen it on her last outing to a combat zone, in Iraq. There a terrorist by the name of Bin Gahli had made no pretensions to being civilized. He had met her in the desert rather than a lavish hotel. He had worn dusty Bedouin rags and the musty odor of the unwashed rather than the expensive clothing and exotic scents of Markocevik—smells so appealing she felt like licking the vanilla-cinnamon aftershave off his cheeks.

Bin Gahli's face, in contrast, had been pocked and pitted, his manner crude and threatening. Not to mention his behavior.

Bin Gahli had threatened to kill her from the moment she had met him through the several days she had known him, and at the last had actually tried to do so after dragging her around the desert like a camel carcass.

This man, Markocevik, had greeted her as if she were a state visitor, giving over an entire floor of the hotel to her and her three-man crew and offering press packets and informational tours of the city, putting bureaucrats at her disposal for background briefings. He had won over her crew with his most recent gesture, creating a media heaven by opening one end of the bar to them and serving all they could handle on the house. Nina had earned her crew's everlasting hatred by turning down the freebie drinks on behalf of them all. Now she noticed her two baboons—Rogers, the engineer, and Autry, the sound technician—were baring their teeth at her from across the room in stupid smiles rather than aggression. She knew they were on Markocevik's tab again. Ritter, the videographer, was probably off somewhere stuffing himself with food, his drug of choice.

She waited, keeping her silence. Not only because she did not know the question he had asked her. But because sometimes a reporter's most effective way to get somebody talking was to keep her mouth shut. A trick that had taken her years to master. Keeping quiet did not come naturally to her. She examined his face, trying to find a reasonable doubt. She did not. By all accounts, he was a cold-blooded killer, the so-called Butcher of Belgrade. Rumor said he had ordered the killing of thousands. Legend had it that he had personally murdered a few hundred. Nothing in his eyes contradicted the stories.

And no amount of silence was going to persuade him to blurt out a confession to war crimes. She knew she was dealing with a psychotic. Good as she was with the mind games, there would be no peeling of his head like an orange. She would just have to use the direct approach, flat out ask to see prisoner-of-war camps.

Fighting had been going on for months, a series of battles raging back and forth across the rugged landscape. The Serbs had won a few, lost a few. They had taken prisoners, surely. If he admitted to that, she would have the right to demand to see them, demand that he prove there had been no war crimes, no executions of captured soldiers. If Markocevik did not admit to taking prisoners, that might be the first step toward establishing that men had been killed.

She came at him from the oblique. "In the fighting," she asked, "how many prisoners of war have you taken in the Republic of Kosovo?"

He squinted at the ceiling. "Several thousand."

She mentally framed her next questions carefully. Carefully because Markocevik's nectar of devils had begun to make her lips tingle.

He said, "You would like to see some of the prisoners, no?"

"Yes." She tried to bite the buzzing out of her lips as she visualized gaunt men staring hollow-eyed at her from behind rolls of barbed wire.

"Tomorrow then," he said.

"What about tonight?"

She wasn't going to buy tomorrow. Didn't want to give him time to stage a phony visit, moving healthy prisoners around to a single show camp.

He shrugged. "Why ruin a perfectly good evening?"

She had expected excuses, reasons why that would be impossible.

She didn't bite. "Are you saying you can't arrange it tonight?" She stared at him.

He met her gaze. "We have camps within an hour's drive of here. Three of them. North, east, and southeast. Choose one." He stood up. "I will change into a field uniform. Tell your crew to dress warmly against the night chill."

He stalked away from the table, leaving her in a state of distress. She wanted to call him back, but how could she tell him that she was merely putting him to the test? She glanced toward the end of the bar where her crew sat, Ritter having joined the other two. He was stuffed, literally, his hands clasped over his belly as if he had strapped a miniature Volkswagen beneath his shirt. Rogers and Autry were slack-faced from drinking.

Now she was going to have to prod them to get ready for an evening of shooting at some cold, damp Stalag 13.

Being a war correspondent was not all glory. All those stray bullets. And the even more dangerous disgruntled staff. One of these days, she decided, she would have to cultivate somebody high up in the military chain of command. Somebody who could get her permission to go on a Force Recon mission with the Marine Corps. So she could do something less dangerous than trying to drag a crew of television slugs out of a bar.

THE WOODS NEAR STIMLJE—0114 HOURS LOCAL

SWAYNE LEFT PETR in Friel's care without a word of instruction. The man's hands bound behind him indicated well enough that he had lost Swayne's confidence. Not to mention the bad-ass tape—friends didn't pull that stuff on friends.

Friel gave the man a murderous smile, as if to say, *Go ahead and run; make my day.*

Swayne retreated to a covered area and waited. He felt a shifting of the breezes and knew that Night Runner had come. He gave the scissors signal with two fingers of one hand after Night Runner crept into the space at his shoulder, materializing out of the darkness. They both shut off their radio mikes.

"Trouble with the guide?" said Night Runner.

"Not exactly. I just didn't want to take any chances. Any signs of an ambush? I mean, besides the trip wire?"

Night Runner gave a two-tone grunt indicating a negative. "If it weren't for the so-called guide, I wouldn't give it a thought. I'd say it was just a booby trap. A random thing. But with this guy, you have to factor in that he might be guiding us into trouble."

Swayne remembered. What was it? Three missions

ago when an international terrorist had tempted them into a trap in the Arctic regions of Canada?

"So what do we do?"

Swayne could feel the Blackfeet warrior's eyes penetrating the darkness, searching his face. Swayne was the one who was supposed to know what to do. Always the one. But ever since the last mission, his confidence hadn't felt quite as seamless. The loss of Gunny Potts. Flinching at the last second when he had a chance to rid the world of one of its worst, bloodiest dictators. Shifting his aim to kill a terrorist—granted, the most terrible of terrorists—so that he could spare the life of his lover, Nina Chase. She had told him what a gallant thing he had done when she'd finally figured out what he *had* done. Gallant, yes. But not cost-effective in terms of the fight against the world's enemies of humanity. The life of Saddam Hussein spared in return for that of a single lousy television reporter? If Colonel Zavello had ever figured out the stunt that Swayne had pulled, a court-martial would never have been enough to satisfy his blood lust. Not even a firing squad would have been sufficient for the Big Z. He would have demanded pain, agony in the extreme, a death of a thousand nicks followed by a shower of cheap aftershave.

But for Swayne, there was pain already . The concern that he might have lost his edge. The fear that his grandfather, Jamison Swayne, might have been right all along to have doubts about his competence as a fighting man.

Night Runner cleared his throat. Swayne wondered how much time had passed. Talk about losing his edge.

"I don't feel good about stumbling around in the dark with our guide," said Swayne.

"And the dog. Or Perfect either. Too many unprovens."

Swayne knew that Night Runner was suggesting a course of action to him. And he wasn't too proud to take it. "You go ahead. Make a circuit. No more than a kilometer in radius."

"I'll take a look at the ground on the opposite side of that trip wire, too," said Night Runner.

"I'll let the others know you're leaving the perimeter, so they don't open up on you when—"

Night Runner sniffed.

Swayne wished he had kept his mouth shut. He could have waited for Night Runner to leave, then told the others. That was routine procedure. But Night Runner's movements would be anything but routine. He was not an ordinary mortal. He would leave the area unseen by anybody, probably including the dog. And he could return and leave as often as he wanted, probably even in full daylight. And never be seen, let alone fired upon. He—

He was gone. Somehow, even as Swayne sat there in the forest distracted, Night Runner had evaded all Swayne's physical senses. He shook his head. Blinked. Ran his hand through the darkness where Night Runner had knelt seconds ago. Nothing but darkness remained.

Swayne turned on his radio mike. Time to report to Zavello. By doing so, he would be telling the other members of the team what—

"Spartan One, report."

Zavello. Swayne cursed himself. Maybe he had lost his touch after all. This mission seemed to be taking its own sweet course, always keeping one tick of the clock ahead of him. Where was that edge of his?

"I said report."

"Dammit."

"You call that a report?"

KOSOVO, THE ROAD TO STIMLJE—0155 HOURS

NINA WISHED MARKOCEVIK would shut his face. Their Serbian SUV, a classy knockoff of a Lexus Rover, had long since left the paved highway that had led south.

Well, south as far as she knew—she didn't have a compass and she didn't have a clue. All that traveling around Iraq on her last assignment still hadn't given her any sense of direction. Which added to her many doubts. Markocevik could be taking her on a wild-moose chase to get to a POW camp that was the single show camp in all the country. The one she had seen on the competing networks so many times before. The one rumored to be full of Bosnian soldiers right out of boot camp and sympathetic Kosovars who'd been paid to sit around looking sad for the cameras.

She had told him she didn't want to go there. That she didn't trust him. He didn't seem to care whether she trusted him or not. Or whether she picked any one camp over the other.

That was what bothered Nina. He didn't seem willing to hide anything. He didn't act suspicious. She had asked to see a camp, and he had said yes. She had asked to see it tonight, and he had granted her wish. He had given her a choice of three camps. She had chosen one, and when he'd given in too quickly, she'd changed her mind and chosen another.

When he'd shrugged and accepted that choice, she'd gone to the third, then insisted at the last minute on going back to the original one. He had chuckled.

"Whatever you want," he'd said.

Trouble was, she didn't know what she wanted. If only he had showed some resistance. Then she would have known. Always push against the resistance. That had been her credo. It was what had made her a success in the biz. If this gorgeous bastard wasn't going to push back against her demands, it could mean only one thing. He had figured all the angles already and was pulling a scam on her. Or worse, there was no news story in this night trip.

Her boys seemed to think there wasn't. The two of them in the backseat of the SUV were the drinkers, Rogers and Autry. They slept sitting propped against each other like two lovers. Ritter had curled up in the cramped cargo compartment at the rear of the SUV. He snored, sleeping off a meal the size of a Knights of Columbus banquet, from the amount he had charged on the CNN tab.

They had been traveling for the last half hour along rutted trails in the deep woods. In a convoy of about half a dozen troop trucks and a pair of less luxurious SUVs.

Markocevik never shut up, pointing out the sights that she could not see. She guessed he was probably trying to give her the names of landmarks, in case she tried to check out his story by looking at one of the tourist maps in her hotel in the morning. If she had chosen a different camp, he would still have brought her to this one. And given her an entirely different set of landmark names.

Pretty tricky.

If that was what he was doing.

"You seem distracted," he said. She looked him in the eye. She remembered Bin Gahli. The man had played a wonderful scam on her in her near-death experience in Iraq, faking that he did not understand English, getting off on all her insults, which she had thought he could not comprehend.

This was exactly the opposite situation. But maybe the same strategy would work here.

"I'd like to ask you some straight questions."

He gave her a smile. Although there were no lights inside the SUV, his teeth fairly glittered, as if they were radioactive.

"Well?" she went on.

"I'm waiting for you to ask."

"Yes," she said. "But will you answer me?"

"Of course."

"But truthfully?"

"Of course."

"But how will I know you're telling the truth?"

The smile, always the sparkling smile. "How does anybody ever know?"

She didn't answer. Couldn't answer.

"Have you ever known me to lie?" he said. "I mean, personally?"

"No. At least—" She bit her lower lip.

"Don't be afraid to say what's on your mind."

That pissed her off. Not because he was being insulting to her. But because he had hit a sore spot—she *was* afraid to say what was on her mind. She didn't want to hear him admit what everybody else in the world suspected of him. She had let herself be charmed, something she tried never to do, not with presidents, not with terrorists. Okay, with Jack Swayne, but only with him. Now she had fallen victim to this beautiful man with the drop-dead-sexy eyes and dazzling smile. She had let herself be seduced by those things when she knew his reputation was that he had the soul of Satan to go along with the title Butcher of Kosovo. She really hadn't asked one tough question, hadn't challenged his stories, hadn't tried to piss him off worse than he had pissed her.

"Okay," she said. "Okay. I admit it. You're too clever for me. So far. I haven't caught you in a lie to me— personally. But I think tonight's the night."

The smile glittered as much as ever. But it had turned wooden. She was glad that she could not see the expression in his eyes.

"You imply that I have lied to others."

"Of course you have. You told other members of the media that your country does not have concentration camps filled with KLA soldiers."

"That was not a lie."

"Then how is it that you're taking me to a camp? One of three in the country?"

He threw up his hands. "You see how my words are twisted? I did not say there were three camps in the country."

"But—"

He shook a finger in front of her eyes. "I said there were three camps within an hour of the city. I let you choose one, then another, then a third, then the first one again. You are the clever one, not me. Too clever by half."

"How so?"

"Like all American media personalities, you try to ask trick questions so that I will stumble. Instead it is you who stumbles."

She felt a twinge of fury. Too much fury, because it made her snap at him instead of asking an intelligent question. "How so?"

"You do not ask the direct question." Markocevik turned from her to his driver and pointed. The driver pulled the steering wheel left, and the SUV lurched off the rutted road onto a two-wheel track.

"You think you are being direct, but that is not so. You are always two or three or a dozen questions away from what you really want to know."

He let her chew on that one a while.

Even with being tossed around the cab, Nina was glad for the chance to gather herself, to collect her thoughts and be ready for him when he gave his attention back to her.

He took a radio hand mike off the dashboard of the SUV and growled at it in his own language. A speaker gave him back a lengthy message, all mumbles, grunts, and slurs mixed with a healthy covering of static interference. Whatever the message, it bothered Markocevik enough to make him sit silent, his eyes closed, as if trying to suppress an outburst by counting to ten. Or was it a hundred?

Nina's fury gave way to fear. To the layman there might be a world of difference between the rough beast Bin Gahli she had met on her last assignment and this suave handsome James Bond type with the bad reputation. But below the surface qualities, she saw the same deadly core.

Finally he opened his eyes and turned to her, sending a chill right to her heart. She had not been able to see into his eyes in the darkness before. Now, like his teeth, the eyes seemed to glow. It was as if she were seeing a cheap special effect in a cheesy vampire movie. Except that this was no fake image of danger. This was the real thing. Nothing cheap about it.

"Do you understand my language?" He glanced into the back compartment of the SUV.

She shook her head. "None of us does. I promise." She felt rattled, and couldn't understand exactly why. Any other time in her past life, she would have—no, she understood perfectly why. Bin Gahli. He had brutalized her to within a half inch of her life, and that nearly shattered life had been saved most ironically by one of the worst killers in modern times, Saddam Hussein. It had shaken her deeply. And no matter how much vacation time she had spent with Jack Swayne in the tropics, she had not yet recovered. She was afraid of this man. She wanted out of this assignment.

"I didn't understand a word of what that man told you over the radio," she said, trying to reassure him.

"I should tell you."

"Oh, no, you don't have to do that. I'm not interested." She folded her hands in her lap. "You know what? I'm not into seeing your little camp either. I don't think I want to do this story after all."

He laughed. It was not a humorous laugh. "But you must," he said. "We have come so far. And since you do not be direct with me, I will be direct with you anyhow."

"Don't."

He wasn't listening. He was glaring at her.

She looked him in the eyes, not in the least ashamed that tears had begun to well up in her own. If tears would

help her now, she would show them. Not showing them
had cost her a lot before. She wasn't ready to go through
that kind of punishment again.

"We could go back to the hotel," she said. "I'd like
another drink of your wine. Liqueur. Whatever it is. I've
already taken up more time than you have allotted to
this interview."

She had come as close to begging as she ever did.
And she could see that it was doing no good. He wasn't
even listening to her. When he spoke again, it was softly.
The bouncing of the truck, the roaring of the engine,
they almost drowned out his voice. But not quite.

"We have a report"—he pointed, and his driver chose
an even fainter trail to the forest—"a report of enemy
soldiers inside our country."

"An invasion?" she said, almost to herself, since he
was preoccupied with directing his driver. She could
only hope. An invasion might mean that he would have
to go back to the capital. Or to some military headquarters to take charge of—what? He wasn't in charge of
regular military units. He commanded the secret police.
Although the country did not acknowledge having such
an organization, because it was too easily connected in
the international press to the Nazi SS. All the implications remained, though. Presidential bodyguards. Inter-
nal security. Ethnic cleansing. Elite unit operations.
Camps. Executions. Terror. Extortion. The works. According to rumors and unconfirmed reports.

Finally the SUV broke into a clearing. Markocevik
directed his driver to stop. He looked at her, one eyebrow raised—she could see it in the reflection of the
instrument lights on the dashboard.

"How do you like it?" he said.

"What?" she said. She looked past him. She had expected to see what she had always seen in the movies.
Concertina wire. Guard towers. Security lights. Bunk-
houses.

"The camp you wanted to see."

"I don't see anything."

He clucked his tongue. "Well, then, I must have lied again."

Her heart hammered inside her chest. She didn't know what was wrong. She just knew that something was terribly wrong.

"You see, my dear, it is true that there are no prisoner of war camps."

"But you said—"

"I said because that's what you wanted to hear. It was the only thing you would believe, am I not correct?"

Nina bit her lip. She didn't want to talk and didn't want to listen either.

He gave her no choice. "To be precise about it, my darling, we have no extermination camps either. Think how inconvenient that would be. In this age of satellite telemetry, a good-hearted country such as your own could identify such a facility before it had even been built to completion. A Tomahawk missile could wipe it out—" He snapped his fingers before her face, causing her to flinch. "A special operations unit might take embarrassing pictures and put them on the international news."

Nina wished she could summon some of that old fire that had been dimmed in Iraq and its aftermath. She'd like to go for the buckle knife she wore, a new one suggested by Jack. One with a three-inch blade. Something conducive to creating actual damage. Say, now. If she would only plunge it into this man's throat. If she only could.

But she could not. She moved her hands to her knees, a subconscious gesture to get them as far away from the weapon as she could.

"Besides, keeping prisoners is such a high-cost undertaking," he went on. "You have the food, the care, the guards. You have the eyes of the world looking on. You have—"

He cocked his head at her. "You are speechless."

"Not really," she said. "I don't see that we have anything to talk about, do you?" She thought it a nice try, the words snotty enough, but diminished in effect because her voice was so weak.

"I don't understand. I thought you wanted a story."

Was he offering her a way out? She grasped for it. "I don't see a story here. Perhaps I was mistaken. Maybe I screwed up. It happens all the time in this business. Let's go back—"

He held a finger to her nose and twirled a dial on the dashboard with his free hand. He spoke into his radio microphone, his words the angry gush of his Eastern European Slavic language. Then he turned to her.

"Yes, let's go back," he said to her.

She heaved a sigh of relief.

She saw the parade of figures passing by the SUV. Men—no, men and boys. They walked into the headlights of Markocevik's vehicle. They were drenched in the soaking rain, most in their bare feet, many in only underwear. All had their hands tied behind their backs. Every group of four was connected by a single strand of cord looped from one neck to the next with a few feet of slack between.

"But first," he said.

"No."

"Yes. You have insisted on getting a news story, and a news story you shall have."

"No. Please, Mikel."

"I hope you don't find it too inconvenient that we will be staging this for your benefit. I know how the networks frown on artificial news events. But I think the content of this story—its pure shock value—will overcome the staging, don't you?"

He climbed out of the vehicle, adjusting his uniform and pulling on a soldier's poncho.

"No."

"Yes. Indeed."

With a few hand signals, Markocevik directed a squad of men to arouse Nina's camera crew.

Ritter wanted to know what the hell was going on. Markocevik snarled at one of his soldiers, and the man raised his assault rifle, turned it on its side, and fired a long burst. The recoil of the gun swept the barrel sideways, mowing down one group of four and a pair of men in another group. Those last two fell over writhing and dragged the two survivors to the ground by their necks.

"That is what is going on."

The CNN camera crew recoiled from the sight of murder. They cursed and prayed in the same exclamations.

Nina was out of the SUV. "No, Mikel, for God's sake. Don't do this. Please—" She reached for him, but he raised his pistol and held her off by pressing the slide against her cheek bone.

"You will witness a news story of unparalleled importance. A story so realistic because it is, in fact, real. A story of incalculable impact because of its emotional impact. And, of course, the impact of bullets."

She put her hands to her face, covering his pistol. She sobbed. No longer was she afraid to cry, and although her tears could not be distinguished from the raindrops falling down her face, clearly she was crying. This was no contest of wills, as it had been with Bin Gahli. Markocevik was trying to place the responsibility for these men's deaths on her. It was cruel, insanely so. She was intelligent enough to know that it was he killing them, not her. And cynical enough to see that once she and her crew had witnessed the atrocity, they could not live to report it.

Almost everyone in this clearing who was not Serbian

was about to die. The Serbs knew it. And she knew it. Even her crew, cursing and murmuring, but to themselves and not Markocevik. They might not know consciously what was going on, but they had to suspect in their hearts that they must die, too. They were now merely going through a phase of denial. A brief phase.

Gently, so he would not interpret her action as resistance, she clutched his hands in hers. Carefully, she turned his pistol.

Markocevik did not resist her. He let the barrel of the handgun be lifted from her face. He allowed his wrist to be straightened.

She placed the bore of the weapon between her eyes and sighted down each side of the pistol at his face.

She had never done anything brave in her life, so the next words out of her mouth she'd assumed to be brave without knowing. "Take me," she said. "Spare the others."

Markocevik squinted at her, his arms still steady, his pistol still pressed to her face. He didn't seem to know what to think of this act of hers. Was it an act of bravery? Was it an act of foolishness? Trickery? "Think of the journalism awards you would win," he said.

With his other hand he held her by the throat, his fingers closing on her scarf, a yard of silk she had picked up in Baghdad on her last near-fatal outing.

"It's me you're angry with. I insulted you back at the hotel. Punish me, not the others. Spare them."

His eyes widened. "Your crew?"

It was the first overt indication her men realized they were in danger, and they renewed their wailing at a higher pitch.

She nodded her head slowly. The pistol wobbled up and down, never losing contact with her skin. "The crew. The prisoners. Spare them. All of them. Take me."

He squinted at her. She could see that he did not know

whether to believe her or not, that nobody he had murdered—and she no longer had doubts that he had murdered many, and personally—had ever acted this way.

Finally, he loosened his fingers at her neck. He undid the silk and slid it from her throat.

His turn to shake his head. "I have never seen such bravery." He put the scarf to his face and inhaled deeply, as if this were a sensual moment instead of a deadly one.

Nina truly wanted to die. But not because she was brave. Rather, because she was too much a coward to have to watch what would come next.

THE KOSOVO WOODS—0216 HOURS LOCAL

PERFECT LISTENED TO his captain getting chewed out.

Pretty damned funny. He had seen some weird things on the movie sets where he had been a specialist, a dog handler with impressive Hollywood credentials in training animals for the big screen. Producers doing starlets. Producers doing stars. Stars doing stars. Stars doing producers.

He could have stayed in the Wood. He might have worked his way up to the top. Hell, all you had to do was let yourself be done. What was the challenge in that?

This was better. You worked your way up with what you had in your head, not what you had in your pants. This was a challenge, a place to work the Perfect con, maybe outsmart the best of the best and go back into the world as a conquering hero. Write a book about the experience. Get a movie made of his life. On second thought—

Forget the book. That was too much work. The movie he could swing. He already had the contacts.

Could he pull it off? Work his way through this crew of chumps and get the Medal of Honor?

First there was Friel. Not much of a challenge because he was a psychotic. Every time Perfect looked into the man's eyes, he saw murder. The Perfect murder. He would use that hatred against Friel someday. He'd own Friel. Make him beg for his life. Let him understand that he'd been had. Then save his life. Maybe.

Night Runner was a different kind of gunnery sergeant. Definitely not old-school. Perfect would rather have a noncom screaming in his face than be given the silent treatment. No, that would be too easy, maybe even easier than Friel. The chief would be tough to beat. He could outrun, outsneak, and outfight anybody. That was his rep. But Perfect had seen the guy make a mistake, missing that wire. He could be beat.

Swayne was something else. He kept everything in his head. He'd have to be outsmarted big-time. Perfect felt he was up to the challenge. No glory worth having was easy. He'd just have to find a way to get the good captain to write his medal citation, even if he did it posthumously. Not Perfect's posthumously either. Swayne's.

It didn't matter that the Marine Corps considered the Spartans the best small-unit fighting team on the planet— in the universe, he thought wryly. This mission didn't require fighters. It needed somebody with superior senses like Gus. And somebody with brains. Like himself. Somebody able to control his emotions. Somebody without a chip on the shoulder. Somebody able to conduct a technical mission that didn't require bloodshed.

In other words, somebody Perfect.

ZAVELLO'S REPORT TROUBLED Swayne more than Swayne's report troubled Zavello. Serbian units all over the country had begun giving indications that their alert status had been increased. Some mechanized units had already begun mobilizing, forming convoys. Aviation units—both helicopter and fixed-wing—had sent out reconnaissance craft.

Swayne shrugged to himself. So what? These maneuvers had gone on before—he'd seen all the intelligence reports for the previous six months. Usually they meant an attack on a suspected resistance group or regular unit of the rebel troops. Sometimes it meant a village would be encircled, its citizens held captive for a couple of days. Then Serbian units would withdraw and streams of refugees would pour from the area. They would be women and children mostly. All the men would be elderly. The refugees would be grief-stricken with hysterical reports of rape and the mass murder of all the young men.

That was why the Spartans had been sent into Kosovo in the first place. To gather proof of the atrocities. To establish reason enough for the international community to be first outraged, then demanding, then insulting, then threatening, then conciliatory, then doubly outraged— the whole string of diplomatic steps that would have to be taken at the cost of thousands of lives before anybody would do something about the killings, no matter how well they were documented, no matter how long they went on during the peace preliminaries.

But Swayne kept these thoughts to himself. He had his job. His team would collect the information, leave the country, and turn over the evidence so the international community could go through its series of feeble protests. By the time anything would be done about it, the Spartans would be on to one or two other events. It wasn't their business to give an opinion about how world affairs should be handled. Just gather the facts, ma'am. Just the facts.

Meanwhile, Zavello ran down a string of possibilities for all the Serbian activities.

"It could be just another mass-murder operation," Zavello growled.

Just another mass murder, Swayne thought to himself wryly.

"But it might also be an operation directed at the KLA." The Kosovo Liberation Army.

Swayne didn't care. From what he knew about intelligence reports from the area, one group was as brutal as the other.

Zavello said, "Or it could be a reaction to NATO forces taking up positions near the borders."

Swayne's mind wandered. This would not concern him.

But the next words out of Zavello's mouth did concern him.

"Or else they have a fix on you."

Swayne's mind snapped to attention. Because of the rocket strike, he would not rule it out, no matter how much faith he had in his team, particularly Night Runner, who could sneak the Spartans across a football field. During the Super Bowl.

He could not rule it out because this was not the same Team Midnight that had gone into Iraq on Event Scenarios 14 and 15. They had lost more than Gunnery Sergeant Potts. They had lost that feeling of measured invulnerability that every special operations team must cultivate. You had to be trained to the knife edge of perfection, eager to the point of anxiety, cocky just short of arrogant.

A team had to believe they were better than the enemy. Or else no team would ever take on the missions impossible given to it by general officers who had long ago forgotten the feel of combat. Ordered by politicians who had never known it.

Swayne knew his men were not afraid. They had not lost their nerve. They had merely gained a sharpened sense of mortality. Fear of dying would not prevent them from taking risks on this mission or any mission to come, any more than too much carelessness had caused them to take foolish risks on any past mission.

Somewhere between Missions 1 and 15 each of them had suffered battle wounds, so they knew they could be hit. Men had come and gone. Force Recon men on other teams had been killed often enough so that everybody in special operations understood how dangerous their lives were. But nobody among the Spartans had died. Until last year. They would have to go through this mission and a couple of fights before each individual sense of confidence, including Swayne's, would be fully restored.

Besides, there was that guide Petr. He was a wild-card factor. Intelligence crews of the CIA had vouched for the man, had shown off photographs of partly opened ditches. But nobody could establish that these were not graves created by the KLA. Only untouched pictures taken by the Spartans would be accepted. And only after DNA tests had proven the race of the victims, if possible their identity, complete with comparisons to living relatives who had already made atrocity accusations.

Swayne's Force Recon Team had never before relied on anybody outside the team. He did not trust the man. And never would.

He did not trust Perfect either. Or the dog. Not that they had given him reasons for mistrust. In training they had performed perfectly, so to speak. Friel, whom he trusted implicitly, had had a much more difficult time fitting into the team's fabric. Not only in training either. On his first few missions he was sloppy and far too sassy. And chatty. But when the bullets started flying, Friel had never let down his mates. All his arrogance he focused on the enemy. He could fight as well as any Marine. And he could shoot better than any Swayne had ever known or even heard of. He was brave under fire and stoic in the face of pain. Swayne could not imagine his team without Friel.

For that matter, without Night Runner. And Potts.

Which made it so hard to accept Perfect. Not only for Swayne but for the others as well. He hoped that Perfect would have the opportunity to prove himself in combat. So the others would accept him. So Swayne could accept him, too.

No sooner had the hope for Perfect formed in his head than a voice spoke in his earpiece.

"Attack."

Perfect again. Giving the signal for imminent danger the second time tonight.

Swayne bit his lip before answering. If the kid was wrong, if this was a false alarm, if this was a betrayal of his loss of nerve, he'd never be accepted by the Spartans.

NIGHT RUNNER FROZE at Perfect's second danger report of the night. Three sensations hit him at once. First and least important, that Perfect had somehow spotted him. Although he had sneaked well clear of the Spartans' position ten minutes ago. He dismissed that notion. Hell, even with the dog's superior senses, he was too far away from them for that to have happened.

Second, the team was facing danger without him? This idea he could not have dismissed. But even as he turned in his tracks to slip back toward his team's position, he was struck with the third sensation.

The smell of diesel exhaust? He turned his face into the breeze and tested the air. Definitely diesel. Acrid and nose-biting. Concentrated enough to have originated less than two to three hundred meters upwind.

He held his position, turning his head so his ears could sweep the terrain like ground-radar funnels, trying to pick up the rumble of diesel engines. Meanwhile, he sorted through courses of action as quickly as he might separate a deck of cards into its four suits.

Hustle back to the team's position? Either join the group for a fight or help them evade?

Retrace his steps and join a fight by hitting the enemy force from the flank or rear?

Check out the source of the diesel exhaust? Possibly identify other military units? Find out if the numbers were too many to get engaged with?

Continue to hold his position? This one troubled him most. He was not used to indecision. But now he was faced with a new problem. Before, he was just a fighter whose responsibility was to be a part of the team and to fight well. Now, an overriding duty was to be a leader for the others.

Some leader, he thought. Welded to a spot in the forest, trying to make up his mind about what he ought to do.

"Two, this is Spartan One."

Captain Swayne. Probably wondering what his second in command was going to do to help the team out of its latest situation. What could he say? That he was paralyzed by indecision, unable to do anything?

Night Runner didn't like this leadership crap one bit. If this was the kind of thing the Marine Corps was going to do to him, he might have to get out of Force Recon. And once out of special operations, he might have to leave the Corps altogether, unless—

"Runner?"

Damn! Allowing himself to be too distracted to answer the radio? Damn this leadership stuff.

AS HE WAITED for Night Runner to answer, Swayne lay beside Perfect and observed the landscape below. It took a while to see what the kid had seen. But when the platoon of soldiers came into view, Swayne whistled under his breath in appreciation. Even without the digital magnification of night-vision binoculars, Perfect had spotted the unit a full kilometer away. Or else his dog had spotted them. Swayne realized a breeze was in his face as he scanned the line of advancing troops. Yes, the dog. What a find for the team. If the Marine Corps could only train other—

It struck him. These soldiers weren't simply on patrol. They weren't combing the woods for signs of an intrusion. They had stretched out on line and moved up quickly. In three overlapping waves. One wave always in position behind rocks and tree trunks to cover the advance of the other two.

He turned up the magnification to 20-power. The image bounced with every twitch of his hands, with every beat of his pulse. But he was scanning anyway, scanning quickly, until he discovered a glimpse of what he wanted to see through the mist.

The unit leader. Wearing a headset not unlike his own, except not as compact. But he saw the antenna and boom mike strapped to the man's helmet.

Swayne turned down the magnification to 15-power and worked his elbows into the mattress of pine needles on the forest floor to steady himself. He saw the man's mouth moving as he gave directions. Or maybe he was reporting to his commanders. But that was not what interested Swayne. Another soldier beside the platoon leader carried a device that looked like a laptop computer. The officer kept referring to it with one finger. Then he would point—although nobody in his platoon could see him except for people standing right beside him—and give directions over the radio.

Swayne's pulse fluttered. The man was pointing directly at him. Sure, still a half mile away, but Swayne had no doubt about it. The unit was homing on the direct line toward the Force Recon Team. Make that the team minus Night Runner. *Night Runner, dammit.* Why hadn't he answered?

"Night Runner," he said for the second time. The

PERLOBEs had been giving them problems almost from the moment they had landed by Stealth helicopter into Kosovo. Had something gone wrong with his radio, too? The last thing he wanted to do was get into the shit without the experienced Night Runner around. The last—

"This is Two."

Swayne relaxed a bit. He had always known that the Blackfeet warrior from Heart Butte, Montana, was a mainstay of the Spartans. But ever since Iraq, Swayne had come to realize that Night Runner was the essence of the team and the main reason for its success. No humility there. Just fact.

Swayne and Night Runner exchanged observations. Friel chimed in to say that a second platoon had showed up on his scope a quarter mile below the one that Perfect had spotted.

"The Mooks are homing on us like we been putting out party invitations," Friel said. "We been laser-painted?"

"Sensors?" Perfect said. "On the ground or in the trees?"

"Our guide?" said Night Runner.

That was Swayne's best guess, too. It was time to get some answers out of Mr. Petr Man, whom he had left sitting at the base of the tree, his ankles strapped together.

He told Friel, "Henry, keep me posted on the bad guys." He pulled back from the crest of the ridge and took a penknife from his pocket as he knelt beside his guide. Or traitor, whichever the hell he was. The man began to struggle against the nylon ties, his eyes wide and glassy.

Swayne held up a finger and drew it across his lips to indicate in sign that he intended only to cut a slit in the bad-ass duct tape. That was one of its amazing features. Swayne had seen the demonstration of the tape

being used as a tow-rope pulling a concrete block the
size of a sofa across damp ground behind a tractor. Until
a NASA scientist stepped up to the makeshift rope. She
held up a sharpened fingernail. With a flourish, she put
the tip of the nail to the tape. It split, snapping like a
gunshot.

"Are you going to keep your mouth shut if I cut the
tape?" he asked the KLA man. Who nodded vigorously.

He barely touched the tape with the tip of his knife,
and the lips flapped opened. But the sound Swayne
heard did not come from the Kosovar but from voices
in his headset.

"Uh-oh," said Perfect, "Gus is acting up. Something
is about to happen."

"Holy shit!" said Friel. "Un-ass the joint. We've got
incoming."

Swayne flattened on the ground. He didn't hear any
sounds of shrieking artillery rounds, and he didn't stop
to listen. Didn't stop to question. He would never take
a moment to doubt Friel. The kid simply did not sound
false alarms.

Yet there was nothing. No sounds of cannons. No
shriek of projectiles. No explosions.

Swayne got to his feet and raised his knife. Petr
cringed. Swayne slashed at the air above him in frustration. He couldn't kill the man in cold blood. Atrocities
were what they were to report, not commit. So he lashed
out with a boot, striking the man in the jaw, knocking
him out. If Petr were a traitor, let him be helpful to the
Free World instead of the terrorist nation of Bosnia.

Feeling his anxiety rise with every passing second,
Swayne rolled the man over onto his belly in a shallow
depression in the forest floor next to a log. Making sure
the man could not see him, he put out a motion-activated
Vid-sensor and looked around to survey the situation.

He saw that Friel had jumped back from the ridge and
had taken off toward the south at a full run. This puzzled

him. If the street kid from Boston had heard incoming, he would have thrown himself on the ground. What was going on, he could not guess. And he knew he did not have time to ask.

Perfect had pulled away from the ridge, too. But instead of running, he was standing with a grip on the collar of his dog.

"Get moving, Perfect," Swayne ordered. Sometimes you could sit around and analyze a situation. Swayne did it all the time. This was not one of those times. You had to know the difference between a time for wracking the brain and a time for hauling ass. As Potts used to put it, "You got to know when to hold them, you got to know when to fold them, you got to know when to make a chowder, and you got to know when to take a powder."

It had always made Friel laugh hysterically. "Gunny, that don't make no sense," he used to tell Potts, who always answered, "Son, the day it makes sense to you, it will scare the hell out of you."

It had never made any sense to Swayne either. Until now. Now it was time to take a powder. He barked at Perfect, and barked again when it didn't seem as if the new man was running fast enough.

Branches hit Swayne in the face. He didn't like running at night. It felt too much like panic.

Swayne had known panic himself. Often. On his last mission, for example, as he lay on the desert floor illuminated by the beam of a helicopter landing light, waiting for his back to be stitched up with cannon fire. And on the mission before that, as he was being dragged along the hull of a submarine toward the screws. Both literally and figuratively.

As Swayne knew he would, Friel came on the air to explain why they needed to clear the area at top speed.

"The bad guys," he said, speaking in bursts. "They all stopped. In place. Hollering at each other. Dropping to the ground. Covering their butts."

Swayne understood. Somebody had warned the advancing troops that a strike was due. He found an overdrive gear and ran with his hands in front of his face.

This was not quite the tangible fear that he had experienced on those earlier missions. But the more he thought about some kind of bomb or missile falling in its trajectory toward the spot they had just vacated, the more real his fear became. Besides, just the act of running at full speed in the dark, chased not by ghosts but by high explosives, stoked his imagination. Which cranked up the panic level.

Somehow the dog called Gus understood the emotions. He went streaking past Swayne, his white-feathered rump held close to the ground in an all-out dash.

Swayne realized he should have patted down the Kosovar to see if he was wearing a hidden radio transmitter. He should have—

The Kosovar. Should he have left the man called Petr lying in the forest?

What choice did he have? Enemy or friend? There was no way to decide. So the team would have had to keep him under guard. Which they could not spare the manpower for. He was better off lying flat on the ground behind the ridgeline. When the ordnance started falling from the sky—

The explosion came with the thought, the concussion slapping Swayne on the back, throwing him in the direction he had been running. He landed softly on an area of the forest floor spongy enough with pine needles to have been a wrestling mat.

He covered his head, fully expecting a complete barrage to follow the first round. The Serbs did not disappoint.

A barrage of airbursts shattered the night maybe two hundred meters short of their position. Bad shooting?

No. The Serb artillery had been laid behind them like the anvil to the hammer of the infantry moving up that hill. For safety's sake, on the far side of the Marines, so there'd be no danger of a stray round hitting among the Serbian infantry. In no time, the rounds would begin walking closer, directed by the advancing troops.

After this volley, he leapt to his feet and hollered, "Rally point Delta. Move out before they adjust fire."

NIGHT RUNNER HEARD gunfire—an assault rifle out of the Eastern European inventory, if his ears did not deceive him. He and the team had gone through enough exercises of listening to weapons being fired in all sorts of situations to be able to make some rough discriminations. The distinctive report of each individual round told Runner that the weapon was the more modern type issued to the elite Serb soldiers of the State Security Force. So far they had not been reported in the conventional Serb Army.

What to do? Of course, he should not have had even to ask the question of himself. Ever since boot camp, he had been trained the simple 3M method of setting combat priorities. Mission first. Then Men. Finally Me.

He set off on a quick pace toward the sound of the assault rifle. He was at the lip of a steep ravine. He remembered the feature from the last time that he had looked at the digital map on the screen of his palm computer. He estimated that he had gotten to within a hundred meters of it when the first reports of troops moving up the ridgeline toward the rest of the team had reached him. He held his position momentarily. The 3M method didn't seem so airtight after all. He could argue to himself that accomplishing the mission was not possible unless he helped the other members of his team out of their scrape.

So he started back for them. Then came the explosions.

New situation, Night Runner decided. His men could hunker down and ride out the artillery attack, if they were already out of the strike zone. The explosions went on, punctuating his thoughts.

If the team did not survive the attack, there would be no reason for him to go back and commit suicide.

If they did survive, they would actually have an advantage for a while. The explosions and flashes would dull the senses of the oncoming soldiers. They might not hear the Force Recon Team running from the area.

Night Runner turned at right angles and moved parallel to the ravine, moved quickly to get clear of the line between where he had heard the gunfire and where the artillery was now hitting. He figured that the diesel smoke might be a military unit sitting in a position, waiting for the order to attack. If so, they would probably move directly—and quickly—toward the beaten zone of the strike. Right at him.

As quickly as he moved, he tried to remain stealthy and quiet. Any attacking unit worthy of the name would have scouts out. He reasoned that the stream in the bottom of the ravine would cover the sounds of his movement. Then again, he did not make much noise even in a strange forest.

He guessed that their Kosovar guide had somehow tipped off the enemy. He would have guessed radio transmitter, except that he had seen the man's hands strapped together behind him. So he could not have made voice reports. He must be wearing a beacon—

The artillery fire had begun walking its way across the landscape. Following the course he had taken after leaving Swayne and the others.

Night Runner knelt and pulled off his headgear, a soft, crushable cap. With the short sword that he had brought out of Iraq, he sliced into the fabric, pulled a button from the cap, and threw it into the ravine. He thought he might have heard a tiny splash as it hit the water. He couldn't be sure. It was one of those moments when even he doubted how good his senses might be.

He wanted to get a report from Swayne, but knew better than to begin asking stupid questions of somebody who was in the middle of being shot at. But he also knew that he had to tell the others of an immediate danger.

"The PERLOBEs," he growled into his microphone. "Drop them in place and clear the area." He didn't even consider turning them off. That would tip off the enemy that they'd figured out the source that was betraying their position. Better to leave the beacons in place on the ground. Let the enemy keep orienting on them, giving the team a little time to disappear into the woodwork of the forest.

Runner saw a spot where a patch of moonlight had bored its way through the canopy and illuminated the slopes of the ravine. He slid down into it, well clear of the spot where he had thrown his PERLOBE away downstream. Just as new artillery rounds began striking the spot. The PERLOBEs, definitely the PERLOBEs.

THE KOSOVO WOODS—0230 HOURS LOCAL

NINA FLINCHED WHEN she heard the explosions. She had learned enough from her experience in Iraq to know that they weren't exactly close, so she did not throw herself on the ground like the three members of her camera crew. She might have joined Markocevik in laughing at them.

Except for the bore of that pistol pressing against the plucked spot between her eyebrows.

Markocevik's amusement told her that he had expected the bombing or artillery strike—whatever it was. She guessed it had been directed at the invasion force that Markocevik had mentioned earlier. It wasn't going to have any effect here. Her life's outcome was going to be decided by this man and this pistol. And soon.

Markocevik kept staring at her. Clearly, he was trying to figure out what was going through her mind before the pistol slug that he was about to send through her mind.

Her camera crew might believe that they were going to get a news story because Markocevik had ordered them to set up their recording and sound gear. But that was simply a ruse.

She thought about the showers at Naži concentration camps. Innocent people were told they were being led there to clean themselves, only to be gassed. The thinking went: *If the captors are sending me to be cleaned, surely they do not intend to kill me. What would be the point?*

But of course, the Nazis would not tell them anything that would lead to mass panic among hundreds of people at once. The showers were just one final lie on top of so many others to keep the masses under control. *That* was the point.

Markocevik would know this. He would be telling Rogers, Autry, and Ritter his story, not so much to control them as to amuse himself. Give himself a great war story to tell later to his cronies. Stupid American television people, he would say. So cynical in their view toward the world. Yet so innocent in believing that they could film atrocities and live to win their awards.

About her, though, Markocevik was not so sure—she could see that in his face as his doubt betrayed him. He lowered the pistol. His eyes kept boring through her, though. Trying to read her thoughts.

So she gave them to him.

I know you are about to kill me, too. I am afraid. I am willing to cry. I am willing to beg. Although I know that neither will do any good. You are going to kill your prisoners. Then you are going to kill my crew. Then you

*are going to mock me. Before you kill me. I am fright-
ened. I want to run. But I know that will not do any
good. Anymore than the begging. Or the crying.*

*So I will smile. It is a fearful, stupid smile. But I hope
it looks like bravery to you. You have killed thousands
of faceless people. You do not remember a single one of
them. Perhaps I can make you remember me. No one
can shame you. But maybe I can craft your worst nightmare with my smile.*

Tears streamed down her face, encircling her silly
fake smile. No, the nightmare just wasn't going to do it
for her. She wasn't going to go out on such a flimsy
hope of revenge.

She hooked her thumbs into her belt. Near the buckle.
Near the buckle knife.

Sooner or later, he would force her to watch the carnage. And because he was a psychotic who probably got
off at the sight of blood, he would have to look at it
himself.

When he did, he was going to get the three-inch blade.

Right in the throat.

Just as Jack had taught her, beneath the ear, slashing
deep and wide.

He might not remember her smile. But he'd remember
the wound. For a while. She could die happy.

She thought about that for a second, as more captives
trooped past her to be lined up and Markocevik's men
brought out two machine guns and began assembling
them on their bipods. This she saw from the corner of
her eye. She was not about to relax her strict eye contact
with Markocevik. If he should indulge a sudden impulse
to finish his business with her by a quick, single shot to
the head, she wanted to die with her image in his eyes,
her image of staring at him in accusation. As best as she
could muster it, that smile dying on her lips with her.

Of course, everything she was thinking was bullshit,
and she knew it. But it was all she had left. It gave her

reason to smile yet again—live by the bullshit, die by
the bullshit.

THE WOODS—0255 HOURS LOCAL

SWAYNE HAD ALWAYS carried his PERLOBE clipped
to the inside of a jacket pocket. Before Night Runner's
warning, he had rolled over onto his back, found it, and
shut if off. His was the size of a pocket calculator—in
fact *was* a pocket calculator, but the LED screen could
operate as a passive receiver like a GPS, too.

Then he thought about what he'd done. If all the PER-
LOBEs disappeared at once, the Serbs would know the
Spartans had figured out they were being tracked. He
turned the beacon on again and threw it into the bushes
about the time Night Runner called to tell them to leave
the beacons on but to ditch them.

He was off and running again, talking into his microphone, ordering Friel and Perfect to confirm that they
had shed their PERLOBEs—while keeping them active—
and were on the move as well.

AT THE SOUND of Swayne's voice, Night Runner's heart
soared like the prairie falcon in a stoop over a partridge.
Coming out of a dive suddenly, swooping at its prey,
forcing air through its wings to make a sound like a huge
shrieking cat, trying to get the bird to fly.

Swayne and the others were all right. They had gotten
clear of the artillery's beaten zone.

He climbed out of the ravine a hundred meters from
where he had gone in. By now, the artillery fire had
begun to concentrate on the spot where he had thrown
away his PERLOBE. As he circled and crept toward the
spot where he had initially heard automatic gunfire, he
marveled at the damage that had been done by the
French, who had stolen PERLOBE technology. Allies

indeed. It had gone from French hands into the terrorist network almost immediately, according to international intelligence reports. And now somebody had developed receivers capable of intercepting satellite transmissions and directing the big guns against American Marines. He wondered how their scientists would be able to overcome and counter that little glitch the next time out. But more important, he wondered if it was going to be safe even to use radio transmitters anymore.

Anybody intercepting their signals might not be able to unscramble their digital-burst messages. But they might well be able to triangulate the source of the signal. And shoot artillery at that.

Those thoughts made Night Runner think of his hand-to-hand battle in the Iraqi desert on his last mission. Two men with knives and that sword. He touched it in its scabbard to reassure himself that it was his now, that he had not imagined the fundamental contest between two men. That short, curved, keen piece of hand-hammered steel had taken on an almost magical quality. He sometimes wondered how it was that he was able to overcome somebody who had slashed at him with it. That he had defeated its owner tended to make him think of himself as immortal.

But in the next instant, thoughts of immortality escaped his head. As the smell of blood washed over him. He knew the fragrance, and not even the rain could wash it from the air. He leaned against the trunk of a huge tree and peeked around it, the rough bark scraping along his cheek. He kept one eye away from the glow and closed besides, to preserve his night vision in case he should have to run away into the darkness of the forest again.

There, in the brilliant white of halogen headlights and harsh glare of trembling camera-mounted lights, stood forty or so men. Lashed together neck-to-neck as he had seen in illustrations of slaves.

Night Runner leaned away from the tree to see through foliage. To confirm what he thought he saw. And realized it was no mirage.

The men were about to be executed. He could see one machine-gun crew, and heard another gun's bolt being charged.

He could see the television crew. His mind would not accept that they were Americans. No matter that the lettering on the side of the camcorder read CNN. A United States television network participating in an actual execution? Cynical as he was about the media, Runner could not comprehend it.

Until he recognized Nina Chase.

But that would be an optical illusion. It had to be. Not two missions in a row.

He lifted his rifle, hitting the on-switch of his nightscope in the same motion. Almost the instant her thermal image materialized on the scope, Night Runner felt a wash of relief.

Even the slightly fuzzy image showed her stress. The trembling came not from his unsteadiness, but hers. She had gotten herself into yet another jam. He shifted his view to the members of the camera crew. They were not filming this of their own accord.

Night Runner's mind took in everything in only a few seconds. His mind raced, and he deduced the ending.

Almost the same instant a pistol shot signaled the start of the slaughter.

WHEN MARKOCEVIK'S GUN went off, Nina stiffened, thinking that she had been hit. But no, he had raised the pistol and fired over her shoulder, striking her only with concussion and powder fragments. That was not enough for him.

Her scented scarf still in his hand, he grabbed her by the hair and turned her forcibly so she had to watch the carnage as it unfolded. As if the triggers of the pistol and the machine guns had been electronically linked, both machine guns went off at once. One started at one end of the file of men. The other gun started shooting at the opposite end.

Noise and images bombarded her. The chatter of gunfire rattling in her ears. Muzzle flashes. Bared teeth of the shooters, grimacing in what could only be called murderous smiles.

Shrieks. Roars. Hollers. Cries.

Raindrops frozen in the flash of guns. Drizzle glistening like silver streaks in the headlights and camera light beams. Splashes of blood washed away in the downpour.

Calls for help. Curses. Prayers. She could not understand the words, only the tones.

Bodies jerked by bullets. Bodies pulled by cords, standing men pulled down by sprawling men. Men falling as the size of the crowd narrowed from end to end. And in the middle of the crowd of victims, men dropping to their knees, some with heads bowed so they would not have to see what was coming. Others with faces raised to the sky in supplication.

She became aware of other sounds. Other men, swept up in the urge to kill, raised their guns and began shooting into the ever shrinking cluster of victims. Growls of the shooters. Grunts from Markocevik—she looked into his face to see if now was the moment when she could go for her knife.

But he was not getting his morbid joy from the deaths of these men. He was getting off at seeing those deaths in her eyes. He had not joined the others in the killing but was looking at her, his pistol still aimed through her hands at her face. Not yet. She could not yet go for the knife. He put the scarf to his face again, to fill his nose with her fragrance—or was it to block the smell of carnage that was filling the rainy night?

He yanked her head back toward the scene of the murder, but she looked past it.

To where she heard sobs nearby. And saw that her camera crew, to a man, was crying. Whether from empathy toward the murder victims or from fear that they would soon join the dead, she did not know. It did not matter.

Then it was over. At least the first round of shooting.

She heard the sounds of metal against metal as guns were reloaded. She heard raindrops pattering as they fell on the SUV. And hissing as droplets hit the steaming barrels of the machine guns.

The men of her crew were gasping for air and choking on their vomit. Ritter kept calling for his mother, but under his breath. Rogers continued to pray. Autry cursed.

And Markocevik grunted as he threw her toward the pile of bodies and waved the damp scarf at her.

She stumbled and fell into the mud. It shocked her that the slime was not cold, but warm. And when she held one muddy hand up to the light of the SUV, she could see why and became sick herself.

Not so much at the gore. But because she had missed her chance. Now, blinded by the headlights, she could not even see Markocevik, let alone kill him. The three-inch knife blade was of no value to her unless somehow she could use it to commit suicide instantly and rob him of the pleasure of killing her.

NIGHT RUNNER PROPPED his rifle in the branches of a tree, the video recording camera turned on and aimed at the murder scene. Then he began running laterally, circling toward the trucks behind the killers, depending on the sounds of gunfire and the horrific sight to keep everybody in the world that might have seen him distracted from seeing him.

He reached the line of trucks and leaned against one to catch his breath and to pull his handheld computer from his jacket. The scientists had told him just how smart this machine was, although no larger than a deck of playing cards. They had programmed features into it that he had sniffed at, knowing he would never need them. Except that now he did need one. Wanted one desperately. If only he could remember the combination of function keys for getting what he wanted.

He did not, his pulse racing hot, his emotions smoking, his rage building to a flashpoint.

He stabbed a finger at the keyboard to bring up the informational menu, found what he wanted, and entered the correct key combination.

The computer wanted to know if his selection was really what he intended.

"Yes, you bastard," he murmured. "Give it up. Now."

The computer wanted to know what level of power he wanted to transmit.

Night Runner, never one to give in to his emotions, felt a scream rise to his throat. He choked it back down and selected high-power, confirmed it, and felt the machine pulse in his hands. It was transmitting. Finally.

He touched the canvas on the truck, tucking the computer into one of its folds.

He turned to run, but somebody grunted at him. Two men stepped from behind the end gate of the truck. He could not understand their language. But he knew from their tone that they wanted to know what in the hell he was doing.

He looked at them, head lowered, as if abashed, checking their posture. Their weapons were slung carelessly. They wanted to know what the hell he was doing, all right. But they did not suspect that he was their enemy. They did not realize that he was their killer.

Until he killed them. With one stroke each from that Iraqi sword he had taken from the vanquished Bedouin. One slash upward, a single motion that unsheathed the blade, struck one soldier under the chin and kept going through the jawbone, dental work, nasal passages, eye sockets, and forehead, lopping off the man's face.

Before the second man could utter more than an angry curse, Night Runner had turned the blade and its momentum, and slashed downward, catching him at the juncture of his neck and shoulder, slicing through collarbone, larynx, esophagus, aorta, and into the man's right lung.

But Night Runner's stroke, strengthened by his fury, did not stop there. It continued. Through the ribs. Through the vertebrae. Through the man's clothing and out the side of his abdomen.

The dead man's knees were locked for a second, and he continued to stand there. Rather, the lower half of his body continued to stand. The upper half slid off along the diagonal slice and fell to the ground. The lower half of the body stood upright for a full three seconds before crumpling.

By then, Night Runner was gone, running into the woods again.

He had disobeyed his orders. He was not to make contact with the enemy, only photograph Serbs committing war crimes. He had killed two Serbs. If the rest of his plan went off as he hoped, there would be more dead. Many more.

He thought he could justify himself well enough. He would have that video. The United States could present evidence of war crimes, complete with video and sound. The fact that a couple of war criminals had died at the scene of their crimes was incidental. Even if they were to discover what he had done, he doubted that he could ever be convicted by a court-martial. There weren't enough men—or women—with combat experience in the United States Marine Corps who would ever convict him.

• • •

NINA HEARD MARKOCEVIK'S voice from behind the glare of headlights. "You wanted to film a killing. Now you have it. You are happy, Nina Chase? Yes?"

She stood up and thrust her chin in the direction from where the sound had come. Defiance. It was how she had lived. It would be how she now died.

Markocevik's men dragged her camera crew into the circle of light. The three were as stiff as mannequins, and probably would have fallen over if they had not been pushed together into a group beside her. The Serbs hit Autry until he turned his camcorder toward the group of shooters.

Nina heard a laugh. Markocevik was amused at the notion of a crew filming their killers at the moment of death.

She heard that single shot again, the signal.

And stiffened her body. As if she could create enough skin tension to ward off bullets. The thought of it made her laugh. It was a hysterical outburst, to be sure.

But maybe it would make Markocevik wonder at her, a woman who could literally smile down the barrel of the gun that killed her.

No, she would not waste her last living thought on that rat-bastard.

"Jack," she cried out over the sound of machine-gun chatter. "Jack, where are you?"

THE FARTHER AWAY they ran from the target area of the artillery, the less tempted Swayne was to turn his radio to the transmit mode. If his enemy had one set of radio frequencies, those of the PERLOBEs, he might possibly have others as well. All Swayne would be able to do from here on out was listen.

During the last event scenario, they had lost all forms of communication. And practically all their weapons as well. It had been an experience to bolster the team's confidence in its ability to fight with low-tech means.

And to navigate using the most effective technology in the inventory, Night Runner.

Now they could use passive means, their GPS receivers. They might not be free to talk to each other or to transmit to the underground center in Quantico, but they could listen to instructions from Zavello in the OMCC, the Operational Mission Control Center. Even if they would have to resort to expedient means again, Swayne felt they were up to it.

He realized that the explosions behind him had stopped. That meant that infantry would soon be sweeping through the area. If the team had left any signs behind, tracks or other evidence of the direction they had taken, a thousand boot prints would very likely obliterate their trail.

He realized once more that footprints were not all that they had left behind. There was Petr.

Swayne felt sick. The man might not have betrayed them after all. Rather, they had betrayed themselves with their own PERLOBE transmitters. And now they had left him in the impact zone of the artillery strike. If he had survived that, he would soon be in the hands of the Serbs.

All this time Swayne had been worried about the Kosovar being a traitor who would get them killed. Petr was the one who should have been worried.

Swayne checked his GPS. Standard procedure dictated what he would find. Knowing their situation, Zavello would transmit a spot for them to rally, sending it earthward from one of the many military satellites above the globe. The blinking point of light on his screen told him where to go after checking for signs of troop movements and factoring in whatever could be deciphered from other means like communications intercepts.

He set an indirect course, but one that would get him there in five minutes.

As he traveled, he heard gunfire. Machine-gun fire.

That worried him because he did not know where he might find Night Runner or whether the sergeant might be the target of that fire. He intended to find out, though. As soon as he gathered up the others.

He found himself in a relatively open space in the woods. First he slowed to a walk. Finally, he stopped. Using his NVBs, he turned a circle in one spot. He saw a hand waving over the top of bushes. And below the bushes stood Gus, his tongue out, panting, smiling his goofy dog smile in Swayne's direction.

As Swayne started to turn again, he saw the distinctive red spot of Friel's gunsight nailed to the second button on his jacket. If it had been somebody other than Friel aiming that beam at him—anybody in the world— Swayne would have known to dive for cover. He turned left, then right. The spot of red stuck to him as if it were glued on. Friel. Definitely Friel.

He made a circle-the-wagons gesture in the air and knelt down to wait for them to close on him. The hard part was over. Getting the two city boys gathered up might be difficult if their electronic navigation devices ever failed them. But now that the three of them were together, they could go anyplace and do anything. No matter where they went or how fast they traveled, Night Runner would find them.

Gus nudged Swayne's thigh and put his head under his hand. Swayne patted the dog's head as he thought of all the possibilities, trying to avoid even considering the notion that Night Runner had been hit or captured.

The gunfire had stopped. Suppose Night Runner had been taken. Suppose somebody had picked up his GPS. Somebody had played with it, accidentally turning it on. Suppose—

Artillery fire started up again.

This time the explosions came from the same area where they had last heard machine guns.

Swayne closed his eyes, squinting hard to focus his reasoning powers. Not an easy thing to do, since Zavello had escalated his tirade, both in volume and venom.

He turned off his microphone and ran through the possibilities. Then it occurred to him what Night Runner might have done. Of course. He had used Swayne's trick from a couple missions ago, in Canada.

Friel leaned in close. "What you smiling about, Boss?"

Swayne shook his head. He hadn't realized he was smiling. Or that Friel had been using his NVBs to study his face.

"You think the chief is up to something?" Friel asked.

"Bet on it," Swayne murmured. "Let's head that way. See if he planted his transmitter in the hip pocket of the Serbs, see if we can lend him a hand."

As they moved out in file, Perfect leading—rather being led by his dog—Swayne realized that the new guy must be feeling left out. Swayne and the other men had come to know each other so well that they could communicate without getting detailed explanations, sometimes speaking only in half-sentences.

He felt bad for the kid, because there was no way to train somebody to pick up on those unspoken signals. Perfect would have to learn it on his own. Swayne didn't have time to teach the kid anything right now. And he doubted that Friel would ever make the time.

That didn't matter. All that mattered now was to get a fix on Night Runner.

AFTER THE SHOOTING had stopped and before the artillery had started up, Night Runner stopped in his tracks to survey the killing ground. He could not believe the surreal scene painted before his eyes like a watercolor washed by the rain and lit by headlights. The bodies lying in tangles. The grotesque expressions on their faces. His incredulity came, not so much at *what* he was seeing—Hollywood had staged executions in films from Westerns to Holocaust dramas to sci-fi thrillers—but *that* he was seeing it. Force Recon Team's mission was to uncover evidence of atrocities. The golden retriever had been trained to find mass graves, so that certainly seemed possible.

On the way into Kosovo by stealth helicopter, Night Runner had wondered how they would ever find a way to connect the Bosnian Serbs with war crimes, to prove that mass graves had been opened and filled with the bodies of executed Kosovars.

Now he was about to witness the reality for himself, on video, from his gun-camera.

Which would show that he stood by, capturing images, doing nothing as murder was committed. How could he have done that? he wondered. Especially now that he realized Americans were numbered among the dead. One American in particular, the woman who held such fascination for Captain Swayne.

Every instinct in his body told him to start shooting, first at the machine-gunners, then at the man in command. And he didn't mean shooting video either. He meant shooting to kill. As they stood there looking over what they had done. He saw the man in charge wave his arms over the fallen bodies. He was directing his men to find the wounded. To kill the wounded.

Night Runner had to get back to his own rifle, which he had left propped in the low branches of a tree.

He found the tree by its distinctive outline. He checked the branches with his hands.

But the gun was gone.

He looked back toward the killing zone. Men lying crumpled and sagged where they had fallen like dominoes, the living pulled down by the dying.

Something struck him in the heart. As if he had witnessed this scene before. No, as if he had lived it. What struck him was grief, and he dropped to his knees to scratch the forest floor, looking for that damned gun.

But it was not there.

How could he have chosen the wrong tree? He took his bearings on the other landmarks in the woods. A dead piece of timber fallen partway, lodged between two upright trees to his left. A clump of bushes that looked like a hedge to his right. Behind him, an uprooted tree forming a disk as if a dinner plate had been stuck into the ground on its edge. To his front, a clear lane to the clearing where innocents were being killed again.

The shooting had begun again. Individual pistol shots. Short bursts of rifle fire. Killing the wounded. He needed his rifle. Orders be damned. He would kill those killers.

As he knelt, he heard a swish through the sky and remembered the computer that he had set to his PER-LOBE frequency. Artillery. He flattened on the ground, only slightly satisfied as the airbursts began striking the Serbian men and trucks assembled at the site of the mass murder.

He felt sick at heart. Of all the innocent people who had been killed in ethnic murder situations like this, these victims were possibly the only ones whose lives might have meant something. They might have died leaving a legacy on video. A legacy that could have been used to avenge their deaths and the deaths of thousands of others like them. Historically speaking, even quite possibly the deaths of those who had died in the Holocaust.

Except that he had failed these people. He had not secured the gun properly to record the killing. It had fallen out of its perch.

Shaken, Night Runner began crawling around the tree. He was aware that men shouted in panic, and some in pain, that they were being struck by artillery fire. Their own artillery fire. He heard trucks starting, orders shouted, men running into the woods, men hurrying down the track that they had made to the forest. But he did not care. He had to have that rifle with its video record. Surely some of it must have been captured before the rifle fell. Surely he was a fool not to have secured the rifle more carefully.

He went around the tree a second time.

Just as the splatter of bullets struck the tree trunk where he had been kneeling.

Night Runner knew better than to merely lie in place as the bullets whacked and burrowed into the tree trunk. Once the shooters knew they had missed him, they would simply lower their aim and tear up the ground where he had dropped out of sight. Then they would begin spraying the landscape all around as if watering a flower garden with copper-jacketed slugs.

So he dove horizontally, hitting the ground hard, and rolled over jagged stones. He felt the pain acutely enough, and realized both his clothing and skin had been torn on the rocky forest floor. But he crawled on all fours, giving up more wounds and leaving behind more blood. And when bullets began snapping through the underbrush above him, he flattened. Still, he did not stop, although roots and rocks clawed at his ribs, knees, elbows, and pubic bone.

Finally, one torn hand closed on a muddy, loose rock about the size and shape of a quarter-grapefruit.

He didn't remember that the forest floor had been so rugged, yet so flat. He needed to find some cover before a stray bullet or ricochet stopped him. He knew what would come next. The firing would let up momentarily, and the soldiers would search for his body.

He hadn't seen a lot of them, but he knew from what he had seen already that they were more professional than the Iraqis on his last mission. They would sweep the area. Once they had a wide perimeter secured, they would light the forest with flares or flashlights and me- thodically search for him. They would find the blood trail he had left from his knees and palms. They would find him.

Still slithering on his belly, the sharp rock clutched in his right hand, he felt the earth lean to the left. He let himself ease down the incline. He wouldn't need much of a depression, a mere six or eight inches.

When he felt that he had gained that much on the slope, he rolled over onto his back to gather himself, to wait, to make his move, the only move that would give him enough time to save his life.

He fingered the stone in his hand. Sharp-edged. But not sharp enough to be obsidian. Flint, maybe. Runner didn't like to think about things like bad luck or his life being in the hands of fate. The two mistakes that he had made tonight—missing the trip wire and moving into a kill zone without ever detecting his ambushers—were just that: mistakes. But diving onto a rocky outcrop of flint stone and being forced to low-crawl over terrain like a bed of broken porcelain toilet bowls, now that was bad luck.

But he didn't have time to reflect on it. His enemy, no matter how sophisticated, was still the human animal, predictable as always.

The firing slackened. Night Runner visualized that his attackers—about a dozen from the volume of shooting— were peering into the night. They would be shushing each other now. They would try to hear what they could not see, their target crying out in pain or trying to flee. If he remained silent, they would be uncertain for a few seconds. He had to suppress a cynical chuckle. Their ears and eyes would fail them. All the concussion and muzzle blasts would have ruined their night vision and set their eardrums ringing. Sporadic artillery fire had not let up. That alone could ruin his scheme.

Night Runner felt the ground around him and came up with two more stones. Above him he saw an opening in the underbrush that gave him what he wanted, a clear angle back toward the tree where the shooting had first begun. The misting rain cooled his face, except for the large drops that fell from the foliage overhead and splattered on his eyelids.

He closed his eyes and waited for complete silence. A muttering followed the end of the shooting. Somebody was giving instructions. There was the clatter of metal as full magazines replaced empties in rifles. He shifted his body.

He held his breath so he could hear.

There it was. A moment between explosions. A second of silence when every ear would be directed toward the kill zone of the ambush. A brief moment of nothingness. He could not wait to act. If they started moving around or if the artillery started up again, they might not hear what he wanted them to hear.

He threw the first stone, then, quickly, the second, a third, and a fourth.

Before they struck the trees, he rolled over onto his belly and braced himself as if getting ready to do push-ups.

The four stones hit the ground in succession, sounding like a combination of boot steps, as if a man were crashing through the brush. Was it loud enough for the deafened men?

The answer was the rattle of one gun. Then a second. Then the cacophony of the entire squad shooting.

This time, though, his enemy was not dispersing its fire to cover an area. This time they were concentrating all their gunfire on that one spot where the noise had come from. Away from him.

But Night Runner did not stay on the ground to congratulate himself. He had to clear the area. Quickly. He moved in that peculiar crouching run of his, keeping low to get as much of an advantage as he could by putting the forest against the skyline. Painful as it was, he moved with his knees high to keep from stumbling over the rip-rap of the forest floor.

His mind working in overdrive, he made an immediate course correction, veering sharply away from the direction his blood trail had sketched over the stones.

Directly behind him lay the scene of the massacre. The thought of all those people dying for nothing took much of the thrill out of the adrenaline rush of escaping an ambush. To his left, less than a quarter mile away, the diesel engines roared through the forest, and artillery moved along behind, pounding the landscape, following the signal of the PERLOBE that he had stuck in the truck canvas.

To his right, he calculated, less than fifty meters away, were his attackers. If he kept on his course, he would slip between the artillery impact zone and the squad. Another course correction would put him on an azimuth back toward Swayne and the team.

The coast, as Gunnery Sergeant Potts might have said, if he were alive, was clear sailing all the way to China.

But Night Runner did not set sail. He dropped to his stinging knees next to a deadfall and stretched out like one of the decaying logs.

Lying on his belly, he crossed his forearms and rested his head. He needed a moment to take inventory. Of the tactical situation and of himself.

Tactically speaking, there wasn't much to inventory. He had failed to get pictures. He had lost his rifle. He had walked into an ambush like a bonehead recruit in boot camp.

As for himself, there wasn't much to be proud of. The Blackfeet warrior and Marine Corps killing machine that he was supposed to be had become as toothless as a great-grandmother. He had not engaged the enemy. Rather the enemy had engaged him and disarmed him. And now the only reasonable path open to him was to E and E, evade and escape. The fighting doctrine told him he should save himself, rejoin friendly forces, live to fight another day. The Marine Corps frowned on maverick behavior and reckless independent actions. You were part of a team, even if that team was as small as four men in a Force Recon Team. Forget your ego. Subordinate your person to the team. That was the doctrine.

Besides, more than living by that doctrine as an individual Marine, he was the team's top noncom. He was responsible for enforcing that doctrine.

Still.

Not to be racist about it, but that was the white man's doctrine.

He had come from a culture that honored the individual warrior. And much of the clash between cultures was written in the blood of the Plains Indian.

He remembered his namesake, Heavy Runner. Respecting the white man's doctrine had gotten him nowhere. Worse than nowhere. It had killed him. If Heavy Runner were given another chance at life, would he have chosen the white man's way? Or the Indian way?

THE PRISTINA ROAD—0312 HOURS LOCAL

ONCE THE TRUCK convoy had rumbled more than a mile from the onset of the artillery strikes, Markocevik realized he had made a mistake. The artillery commander had made a mistake—the entire Army was about to make a huge mistake that could bring down the country.

He had assumed that some enemy in the area had directed the artillery strikes by observation and adjusting fire. He continued to believe that as he drove down the road—any lieutenant of artillery could read a map and calculate targets in the blind. But nobody on the ground could do to them what was happening now. The artillery continued to follow the trucks down the road, adjusting closer and closer—

—an explosion in his rearview mirror was followed

by a slashing of headlights across the sky. The truck behind his had been hit. It crashed into a slope, rolled up sideways, and fell over on its back like a dead roach.

He grabbed his radio mike and began shouting in his own language. "Turn off the artillery. Turn it off now." He ordered his drivers in the convoy to speed up.

It would take a few seconds for his words to filter down as commands to the gun crews. After that, there would be artillery rounds in the air for a few more seconds. If they didn't outrun—

The flash lit up the road ahead of him, and Markocevik shouted for the convoy to stop and turn off into the woods to the right and left of the road.

His own driver turned too fast and almost rolled the truck. Somehow the vehicle bounced back after nearly tipping over, and plowed into the underbrush of the forest.

"Slow down, you fool. Stop it here."

Markocevik jumped out of the truck. So did his men. They ran away. He did not. All he wanted to do was listen.

But he could see, too. And what he saw was one of the drivers who had not gotten the word, continuing to drive down the road.

The exploding ordnance went off ahead of that truck, close enough for the shrapnel to shatter the windshield. Markocevik saw that the driver had been wounded, if not killed. The truck was not being driven anymore. It rolled on its own momentum, its right front wheel falling into a crater in the roadbed. In slow motion, the truck leaned forward, and laboriously lowered itself on its side like an elephant getting down to bathe in the dust. As the truck continued to roll, men poured out of the canvas, trying to jump clear.

They were standing, kneeling, and lying on the roadbed when the last of the artillery rounds struck them. They were barely visible in the pale light anyhow, but orange flame and black smoke enveloped them.

And Markocevik knew. Nobody had been directing artillery on them. Somehow a transmitter had been placed on that truck. Somehow the Americans had arranged for his own artillery to try to kill him. They had not succeeded, of course. But they had gotten him away from the spot where he had left the most valuable prize in Kosovo. That CNN videotape.

He could still hear trucks driving into the forest, and nearby, men continuing to run away, although no artillery had exploded for the last minute. He hollered once, with the handset of his radio keyed, and loud enough for those around him to hear as well. "The firing has stopped. Get back here. Everybody assemble on the road—I want the unit re-formed at the spot where the truck is burning. Anybody who does not assemble at the spot within ten minutes will be shot for cowardice."

SWAYNE WANTED TO use his radio, to talk to Night Runner. To hear a status report. No, more than that, he merely wanted to hear Night Runner's voice. He needed to know the man was alive. But the sound of rumbling, whomping artillery strikes a mile or more away kept him from breaking radio silence.

If the Serbs could pinpoint his position by identifying his radio signal, the rounds would shift to the spot where he and Friel and Perfect had holed up. Or worse, if Night Runner transmitted, he might get hit.

Swayne knew he could not let his emotions rule him. Night Runner could take care of himself. Swayne was responsible for taking care of the other two enlisted men. Better than he had taken care of Petr, his Kosovar guide, a voice inside reminded him.

At the reminder of the man lying on the forest floor, his wrists bound, Swayne felt a twinge of guilt. By now the Serb platoon had made it up the slope. They would

be searching the area where he and his men had left their
PERLOBEs.

He had left a video sensor on the spot, a tiny camera
with its own transmitter. The device would collect an
image day or night, depending on the light. At dark it
operated on the principle of night-vision goggles, collecting ambient light. Its compact batteries, developed
by NASA for the space shuttle, could store enough
power to run the device for eight hours. By day the
camera switched to ordinary digital video. Powered and
recharged by a tiny solar panel, it transmitted a live signal rather than recording on tape or disk.

It might be transmitting now, attached to the tree
where Swayne had left it. He took his palmtop computer
from his jacket pocket and turned it on. Finding the frequency of the satellite overhead, he brought up the image.

Small as it was, he could not see anything of value.
The video camera's default setting was wide-angle, to
give maximum coverage. The device would detect motion, and a flexible prismatic mirror in the lens would
change shape. The effect was to zoom in on the area
where the motion occurred so the camera itself did not
have to move, only the mirror in the lens, which was
the size and shape of an eye in a pan trout.

It did not take long for Swayne to have his answer
about whether Petr was a traitor. The camera's lens
found movement. A group of combat soldiers stood
around the man lying on the forest floor. Swayne could
hear the language, although he did not speak it. So he
pushed the function key on the laptop that would record
the conversation for later interpretation.

He could understand the body language and activity,
though. An officer knelt beside the Kosovar to get a
closer look at the tape on the man's face. He tried to get
a fingernail under an edge of the tape, but could not. He
shrugged, gave a command, and made a hand motion

that made Swayne cringe. A second soldier put a knife blade to the corner of the tape. Petr squirmed in pain and hollered. The soldier did not care. He shook his head and dug at Petr's face. The Kosovar began to heave and twist. The officer kicked him in the head. Two soldiers put their boots on him to keep him in place.

The soldier with the knife struggled with his captive and began digging away. His back was to the camera, blocking the view, but Swayne knew what was going on. He knew from the screaming, which needed no interpretation. The Serb, unable to move the tape, was cutting off Petr's lip in the effort.

The Serb officer saw that he was going to lose a source of information. He called off his men, and they stepped away.

Swayne could hardly look at the screen, which showed Petr's upper lip flapping like a bloody bandage.

The officer shouted at Petr. Swayne knew he was demanding to know where the Marines had gone.

Petr sputtered something and tried to roll over to point. Swayne shook his head. The Kosovar was trying to direct them away from the trail the Marines had actually taken. Swayne felt the prickly heat of shame.

The officer needed proof. So he kicked Petr in the kidneys. Petr tried to shriek, but the pain was so sharp it wouldn't let the man release his breath. Again he tossed his head, again in the wrong direction.

The officer wanted to be sure. He pulled a pistol and shot Petr in the upper thigh.

Petr repeated himself in the body language of his agony.

The officer shot him in the head.

The video's mirror flexed, following the Serb soldiers out of the field of view in the direction Petr had indicated.

After the sensor could no longer detect motion, it shut down to save on batteries.

"Bastid."

Startled, Swayne flinched. He had not heard the kid from Boston creep up on him until he spoke in his clipped New England accent.

"Friel. Aren't you supposed to be on perimeter security?"

Friel half-turned. "Cap'n?"

"Yes, Henry."

"We gonna make them pay for killing our man like that?"

Swayne shut off his laptop without giving Friel an answer. He would keep the image file saved in the computer's memory. Turn it in as part of his post-mission report. The debriefing would address ways Forced Recon teams could train to test indigenous guides to see if they were telling the truth. A review panel would second-guess Swayne from top to bottom on the way he'd handled the Petr situation. Even if they found him at fault, which they probably wouldn't, he would be given a clean slate. But that didn't make Swayne feel any better.

War was worse than hell. It was chaos. Full of twists of fate and accidents and flat-ass mistakes. Petr was an unlucky casualty. The Marines couldn't afford to prosecute the men who went on such dangerous missions, couldn't afford to second-guess their combat decisions made under the stress of battle. If they did not commit outright war crimes or were not guilty of criminally negligent behavior, they would be counseled and sent into training for the next mission. Always the next mission.

The prosecution was left to Swayne, self-inflicted. For he could never forgive himself. Nor would he ever forget that he'd had a hand in Petr's murder. A voice from deep inside told him to shrug it off. But that voice was soon drowned out by a scratchy, whining Southern accent that chided him. Senator Jamison Swayne. His grandfather. Telling him he was in the wrong business. Always speaking up to say at the appropriate moment what Swayne suspected himself might be true.

Swayne's first reaction was to give Friel a thumbs-up, turn back on his track, and set a fresh course to intercept the Serb platoon. Friel shifted from foot to foot as if he had to pee. He wanted an answer. No, he wanted only one answer. He wanted permission to kill the Serbs, wanted Swayne to give him the go-ahead to set off now. Time was passing. All Swayne had to do was nod.

He shook his head, and Friel slumped.

He felt the sergeant's eyes studying him as if looking for an explanation. Or maybe he was giving him an accusing stare. Swayne did not respond.

But Friel wasn't backing down. "We just gonna sit here? Wait for the war to happen without us? I hate that shit. Let's track them down and give them something to chew on."

It was Swayne's turn to stare. Friel's words and tone verged on insubordination. Swayne didn't want to put the man down. Not in the field. But he wasn't going to take any of his smart-mouth either. Swayne glared, hoping the sergeant could see enough to back off.

Neither man moved. Until Swayne had had enough of even the insubordination of silence. He opened his mouth.

Friel could see well enough to see that he was about to get chewed out. He turned on his heel and went back to his spot on the tiny perimeter.

Swayne shook his head. In his heart he thanked Friel for being a smart-ass. If the kid had not spoken up, Swayne might well have ordered the group after the Serbs. As an idea it sounded pretty good inside his head. As a thought, it cried for being turned into action. Only when it came out of Friel's mouth as a suggestion with Friel's murderous backing did Swayne realize how wrong such a decision would be.

They had their orders. They were not to engage the enemy. Already they had been discovered in-country.

No sin in that. But they still had their primary mission. To get evidence of Serbian atrocities. In the memory of his palmtop computer, he had that. The brutal killing of Petr. No matter that Swayne might have contributed to that killing. He had not pulled the trigger. A Serb had. And now he had captured that Serb as an electronic image committing murder. A war crime. A single man and a single killing did not prove a national policy of atrocity.

But it was a start. Sorry as he was for his own mistakes, he would have made an even bigger error to go off on a killing mission. Even if the team wiped out every single member of the Serbian platoon, he would have only satisfied Friel's blood lust. Make that his own blood lust. The team, the Marines, the country would have nothing of military or political significance to be brought home.

Clearly he had to get his team back together. He could sit and wait for Night Runner to find him. Or they could move in the direction Night Runner had taken and, again, let him find them as they were on the move—for the Indian brave was not going to be found unless he wanted to be found.

Swayne called his men and dog together to give them a briefing. Before he had finished, he was interrupted by the sound of gunfire.

The mad-minute of shooting worried Swayne. The pace of the gunfire was even more urgent than what he had heard earlier. A squad, from the sound of it, had found a target and opened up on it. As the shooting continued unabated, Swayne relaxed a little. If they had made a confirmed kill on Night Runner, they would have stopped shooting after the first fusillade. So they were unsure of themselves. He could not make out any return fire, and did not hear any of the boomers go off, the concussion grenades that Night Runner and every member of his team carried with them. They had used boomers on almost every previous mission to get themselves out of a jam. Night Runner would not let himself be taken without resorting to boomers.

When the shooting tapered off, Swayne visualized what was happening a half mile away. The men were trying to assess whether they had actually killed anyone. When the shooting started off again, again urgently, it could mean that they had seen Night Runner and were trying to finish him.

Swayne chided himself. Seen Night Runner? What a ridiculous idea. No, Night Runner had slipped them. They were shooting at phantoms.

Swayne checked his digital compass, which used satellite signals for directional readings, and set it.

He made his decision. He would move the team toward the last gunfire he had heard. Night Runner would find them. If they got lucky, the enemy might find them, too, and Friel would get his wish, would be allowed to kill somebody. To Swayne that didn't sound like such a bad—

"Spartan One, Eagle One."

Zavello. Swayne couldn't answer. The radio silence.

"Eagle One transmitting in the blind. Advisory follows. Source: November-charlie-alpha."

NCA. The National Command Authority. Orders from the President.

"Terminate Event Scenario 16. Extricate Spartans ASAP. Operation Silver Anvil commences effective zero five hundred hours, your time. Rally point lima-yankee 303."

Swayne bit his lip. They had just been ordered to move out of Kosovo. By the President, no less. The rally point lay across the southern border inside Macedonia, or to be accurate about it, FYROM, the Former Yugoslav Republic of Macedonia. About twenty miles away.

He checked his watch. 0401 hours, four hours and change after midnight, leaving about an hour to travel the distance. Not an easy trek at night with half the Serbian Army on the alert for them.

Not to mention that he would have to gather up Night Runner before he would even consider leaving. Force Recon did not leave their comrades—dead or alive. He cringed at the thought. All that they could carry out of Iraq on the last mission was Potts's foot.

Not to mention Operation Silver Anvil.

Face it. They were going to have to dodge bombs.

He saw Perfect and Friel paging through screens on their handheld computers, looking for the code page that would identify the Silver Anvil contingency and the location of all rally points, including GPS routing assistance to get there.

Swayne didn't need to look it up. He was a student of politics because he had always followed the career of his grandfather in the Senate, including his rise to second chair on the Armed Services Committee.

So he had studied the list of possible contingencies before even giving his operational briefing to Team Midnight. From what he knew of the world situation and tendencies of the Administration, Silver Anvil was not merely a possibility, but a likelihood.

"Holy shit!"

Swayne cleared his throat, the tone a warning to Friel to keep his mouth shut. Even so, he heard Perfect groan. Both men eased over to Swayne's position because they knew he would have to brief them. The Spartans were going to have to move quickly. Marry up with Night Runner. Get the hell out of Dodge.

Friel couldn't contain himself, making an opening statement of obscenities.

"Hold it down, Sergeant," Swayne said.

"They're going to start bombing this place off the face of the map?"

"It would seem so, Henry. That's what Silver Anvil is."

"Without even freaking giving us enough time to clear the area?"

Swayne kept his silence.

Perfect spoke up for the first time. "They're going to do a massive bombing? In the blind? Wouldn't it be better if we stayed in Kosovo and helped them by directing strikes?"

Swayne nodded. The kid was quick. Yes, it would have been better from a tactical—with the right target selection, even a strategic—point of view. From a political standpoint, it could not happen. The Administration didn't have the guts. It was the one issue on which he and his grandfather agreed, perhaps the only issue in their lives. This President wanted to play international politics as if it were a video game. Entirely bloodless, clean, painless. In fact, the very kind of war that Lyndon Johnson would have liked to have had in Vietnam. In fact, what Johnson had tried to have with his surgical strikes and no-fire zones and bombing halts and high-tech battle management techniques that included two-star generals directing the combat action of squads and platoons on the ground as the generals flew above the battle in their helicopters at fifteen hundred feet. In fact, the very set of policies that had killed Swayne's own father in that war.

In this war, this President wouldn't allow U.S. Marines to be captured and held hostage, displayed to the world press. Too embarrassing. Combat had become an international struggle of public relations and world opinion. Hell, in this world, it didn't even pay to embarrass your enemy too much. If he could not save face, he might become more desperate. More brutal. As if the Serbs could outdo themselves after the crimes that had already been reported.

Swayne told his two men as much, leaving out the curse words that tasted so bitter at the back of his throat.

"They freaking gonna bomb us?" Friel said. "They

gonna let us be paraded down the main street of Belgrade dead?"

Swayne didn't respond to the incongruity of corpses parading.

Perfect answered for Swayne. "A couple of dead bodies aren't near as bad as hostages, Friel."

Friel spewed some venom about that. But soon he turned his mind to the same thing that concerned Swayne.

"Night Runner," he said. "We're gonna go after the chief, ain't we, Captain?"

NIGHT RUNNER KNEW all the stories about Heavy Runner, his raids against the Crow, Cheyenne, and Sioux. One story, he wished he did not know. The story of his death.

In Montana. At a bend in the Marias River. At a place where the Baker Massacre, a war crime of another century, had occurred. Soldiers under the command of Major Baker had traveled for three days to the bluffs overlooking the winter camp of a band of Blackfeet. They were to arrest Owl Child, who had murdered a trader who just happened to be a friend of General Phil Sheridan. They were to engage the troublesome band of Mountain Chief, who had sheltered Owl Child. Their orders were: "Strike them hard."

But when they arrived that January at dawn in temperatures far below zero, their guide saw that the chief's lodges he had found several days earlier on a scouting trip were now gone. He called to Baker, "Don't shoot, Mountain Chief is not here."

Baker was livid. "If he makes another sound," he commanded, "shoot the son of a bitch." Then he ordered his men to open up on the sleeping village.

Runner had made his pilgrimage to the spot. Had stood on the bluffs overlooking the site. Had taken the point of view of the soldiers who had fired down into the helpless village with heavy-caliber rifles. On the

130th anniversary he had gone down into the Marias River valley before sunup to try to experience what Heavy Runner had felt that morning. It was not easy to do. First, it wasn't cold enough—only twelve degrees below zero instead of the forty below on the day his namesake had died.

The floods of 1964 had changed the river's course, so the curve in the bank was dry. Because the Corps of Engineers had dammed the river a dozen miles to the east, the bottom had been cleared of trees.

Runner found the spot where Heavy Runner had likely walked out onto the ice, waving his peace papers. Moments before a .45-caliber rifle slug had pierced his chest.

Runner stood there, waiting for the sun to rise, watching the fog of ice crystals begin to catch the early-morning rays, watched them glitter and sparkle, covering his shoulders like glass dust, collecting on his eyelashes.

He waited, hoping to connect with the spirit of Heavy Runner. Would he hear the shot, could he feel the pain, could he talk to the spirit of the legend that had died here?

He stood an hour on the spot without moving.

Nothing.

Not a sound penetrated the fog. Not a hint from the spirit world.

Night Runner was worried that he might not have purified himself properly. He feared that he was not worthy. His neck, weary from looking up at the bluff where so many rifles would have been aimed at him 130 years ago, began to ache. He lowered his head. He stared at his oiled, insulated boots. Then it occurred to him.

He was dressed in two-hundred-dollar Danners lined with Gore-Tex and Thinsulate. Layers of fleece insulated him beneath a North Face parka. High-tech underwear. Face mask. Space Age gloves.

He saw that he was no Indian at that moment. How

could he hope to connect with the people who survived temperatures twenty-eight degrees colder than this dressed only in what they could carry from their bullet-riddled lodges?

He pulled off his gloves, tore off his face mask, peeled the parka and layer after layer of clothing. He tossed away his boots, woolen socks, and synthetic foot-liners.

Until he stood stark naked in the bitter air, until he could feel what his people had felt here.

Still it wasn't enough. He turned his back on his clothing and walked away. Half a mile to the north, the new course of the Marias snaked through the valley beneath a foot of solid ice. Barefoot, he began walking toward it.

He had heard about men who taught a brand of commercial bravery by inviting people to pay thousands of dollars for the privilege of walking across hot coals. Let them try this. Before he had traveled a hundred meters, his feet felt frozen to his ankles, although the snow was only an inch deep.

Only they were not frozen enough for Night Runner, because he could still feel pain from every stone and twig on the old river bottom, as if somebody were pounding his soles with ballpeen hammers at every step.

The chill air tried to suck every ounce of warmth from his body. There was no wind except for what he created by walking, yet he felt as if he might be in a wind tunnel.

His extremities were the first to grow numb, as the blood collected at the warm core of his body. His ears, his fingers, his genitals stung; then the feeling left.

He tried jogging to increase the blood flow. He worked his fingers and cupped his hands over his ears and his crotch in turn to bring feeling back.

Halfway to the river, he began to understand his people. That insight came from the feeling of panic that he might not survive this experience without severe frostbite. He might lose some of his body parts. He was risking his career in the Marine Corps—no Force Recon Team wanted fighters without fingers, ears, toes, and penises.

He knew he could turn back. Half a mile away lay his clothing. Nobody would be shooting at him. He could walk away, and nobody would know that he had pulled such a dangerous stunt. But he would know it and a lot more, namely that he had quit. A few minutes of discomfort, and he had quit being an Indian, had put back on his white man's clothing.

Had quit being an Indian. Quit being an Indian. Quit being an Indian. Quit being an Indian. Quit being an Indian. Quit being an Indian.

And that he could not do.

He put the option out of his mind and sped up his pace from a jog to a lope.

Originally he'd intended to reach the river's bed and turn right back. He did not. He had to free himself of demons, felt he must wash his body of whiteness.

It had taken him fully ten minutes to pry a boulder from the river's bank at a spot far above the waterline—he could never have removed it if it had been frozen in mud. He carried the twenty-pound stone to a spot in the ice where he could see the darkness below the cut-bank.

He threw the stone down, and it bounced back toward his feet. Dancing away, he returned and knelt on the ice. Over and over again he brought the stone over his head and pounded it down, throwing chips until the spot was cracked and crazed like a bag of crushed ice. Still he kept pounding the stone, feeling his body heating up except for the spots on his knees and the tops of his feet as he knelt. He felt anger, frustration, grief for people he never knew but whose plight he finally understood. He wanted to cry out. And he wanted to cry.

He scraped out the crushed ice and continued pounding in the depression he had created until, with one last powerful heave, the boulder shot through the ice, creating a spot like a huge bullet hole through safety glass. Water and crushed ice welled up into the hole.

Desperate to cleanse himself now, Night Runner stood up and plunged feet-first through the hole, raising his arms above his head, feeling the sharp edges of broken ice scrape his ribs and arms as he went through.

At the last second, he turned his fingers out and caught the edge of the hole so he would not be swept under the ice.

It astonished him that the water felt so warm. Then again, he thought as he prepared himself to escape an icy death, why not? Water was not water if its temperature was below thirty-two degrees. Outside, his body had been working in temperatures forty-four degrees colder.

Either way, though, he could not stay here. He did not have the air. And face it, hypothermia would kill him, either in the water or outside. As it had killed so many of his people.

So he raised one arm high into the air through the hole and worked his head and shoulders out.

It occurred to him that he had blundered, of course, the instant he opened his eyes and saw that water that had splashed from the hole was already frozen on the ice. He would be tacked to the top of the Marias River, held as tightly as if his body had been coated in Super Glue. He would die. To recover his body, they would have to scrape it off the river like cleaning a bug off a windshield. They would laugh at him. They would wonder what kind of perverted stunt he had been pulling. What would the Marine Corps—

He did not care. It did not matter what others thought of him. It only mattered what he thought of himself. Besides, he did not plan to die here.

Wedging himself at the hips into the hole, he reached out and planted both hands into the crushed ice around the edge of the hole. He kept patting the ice fragments until his palms were completely coated. Then he lifted himself so that he could get a footing, his feet inside the depression that was filled with water. Three feet away a dusting of snow covered the ice. He bent his knees, feeling the joints creak like a rusted car door hinge. He leaped out, lost balance as his feet slid, felt tacky contact between water pouring off his body and the ice below the snow. He kept moving, kept coating his feet with snow dust, until he felt confident he could make it to the frozen ground, which was not nearly as threatening as the frozen river.

Other problems that he had not considered immediately began to crop up. Ice froze in a sheet all over his body, the crackling shards resting against his thighs and poking him in the genitals. His fingers kept wanting to stick together in mittens of ice. His eyelids stuck shut, and he could not warm them with his hands because they were not warm. So he had to rub and break off the ice, tearing at his eyelashes until he could see where he was going.

He found his clothing in the pile as he had left it. And he dressed as well as he could, considering that his fingers would not work to tie knots, zip zippers, or button buttons.

When he had dressed, he could not feel the clothing against his body. Instead, he felt as if he were coated in broken, stinging glass. Ahead of him stood the bluff like the wall of a fortress. He was weak. He could not climb it straight up. He would have to take the long way cross-slope, maybe finding a game trail that would take him back to his SUV.

He started to climb, but could not keep it up. His legs were too heavy. His body did not respond. He was too sleepy. He knelt down to rest. The insulation of his clothing had kept in his body heat and melted the ice. So, he was wet. Once the heat he had generated from his run began to fail him, he would chill at the core of his body. Again he faced death.

He stood up, grew dizzy, the slope leveled out, and suddenly he realized that was because he had begun falling.

When he hit the ground, he was glad that he had lost all feeling in his extremities because it did not hurt. Later, he guessed, it would hurt. But now it did not.

As far as he knew, he never stopped falling, never stopped bouncing off the slope, never came to rest in the dry river bottom. He just kept falling. And falling.

All he knew next was the sound of a voice deep and mocking.

"That was not brave, but stupid, Night Runner."

Beneath his face mask, Runner tried to answer. "Yes, very stupid." The sound of his own words came to his ears as mush.

"A warrior need not kill himself to prove himself a warrior," said the voice.

Night Runner realized where he was, in a remote area where nobody could know his name, let alone his mission in trying to understand his people.

He thought to open his eyes, but the mask had shifted on his face, and he could not see. He struggled to get to his knees, pulling at the mask, once again tearing it off his head. Still he could not see who stood before him, only a figure against the sun to the east. A tall figure, square and wide.

He rubbed at his raw eyes, but that only made it more difficult to see for the moment.

He felt a hand on his head. Was this a dream?

The hand clamped down on him as if giving him a blessing—or maybe trying to force some common sense into his head.

Slowly, tentatively, Night Runner raised his hands toward the sky as if praying. He put them behind his head and removed his high-tech gloves. Then he slowly put them together on top of a bare hand. It was no dream.

"Who are you?" he asked.

The figure did not answer him. Night Runner held the hand on his head with his own right hand and probed up the arm with his left. His fingers closed on long hair, soft and thick. The feeling had returned, so he knew it was not human hair, more likely fur.

"It does not matter who I am. It matters only who you are. You are a warrior of your people. You do not prove this by killing yourself. You prove it by killing your enemy."

The hand came away from his head. Night Runner tried to hold it, but he was not strong. His left hand closed on the robe, but he could not prevent the man from leaving. The figure walked toward the sun, and was gone before Runner's eyes cleared enough to see.

Runner found his feet and decided to follow the man.

But the stranger had left no tracks in the snow. Runner walked a small circle. No tracks but his own, those from falling down the slope, and those from earlier when he had stood in the drying riverbed at the spot where he thought Heavy Runner might have died.

He checked the sun and realized that, of course, he had stunned himself in the fall and lain there for better than an hour. Yes, he had hallucinated. And if he did not get out of this valley, he would die in the cold. Hypothermia was no vision, but a reality.

He rubbed his nose and took a step toward the slope. He remembered his gloves. And his face mask. His nose tickled, and he fought off a sneeze.

Shaking his head at how realistic was his dream, he pulled on his left glove, then pulled it off and stared at his hand in astonishment. Woven through his fingers were patches of hair. Brown, fine, long, and curly.

He had seen it before. In the lodges of the old ones, on the robes that decorated the walls and floors.

Buffalo robes.

His fingers were covered with the hair of buffalo robes.

NIGHT RUNNER, LYING on the floor of the forest in Kosovo, with no weapon but the Iraqi sword and a survival knife in his boot top, feeling sorry for himself because he had lost his weapon and the precious pictures, decided. It had been no dream that day in Montana. It had been a vision and then some. Heavy Runner had spoken to him. All that he'd needed to know about himself, he had been told: He was a warrior. A warrior did not run away from a fight.

What would the white man say about his failure to obey orders? What could he say? The mission was to get proof of Serb atrocities. The video camera mounted to his rifle had that proof in it. Night Runner was merely recovering the evidence. Attacking his enemy was a by-product of the mission. That was what he told himself. It wasn't much, wasn't even true. But it was enough for him.

He crouched and pulled the deadly sword from its sheath. And, the words of Heavy Runner fresh in his ears, he slipped like a shadow into the forest. Toward the enemy that had tried to kill him.

PRISTINA ROAD—0421 HOURS LOCAL

MARKOCEVIK TOOK STOCK of his force assembled by the eerie glow of the burning truck. He had lost half his trucks altogether, some back at the execution site, two in the escape attempt, and two more in the forest—one had crashed into a tree, another had fallen into a creek bed.

His men had not fared even as well as the trucks. Some had apparently been killed in the first artillery strike, others had been maimed in truck accidents, and a few had been cut to ribbons by shrapnel from their own artillery. It had been a lightly armed force anyhow. He had called for them on short notice to teach the woman from CNN a personal lesson in brutality. He had told his officers to gather men and ammunition, plenty of extra ammunition. They had understood what was to be done. They had known that they needed men who could keep their mouths shut, that the only extra equipment to carry would be rain gear. And brandy for the ride back home, to get the taste of killing out of their mouths, to dull the sense of smell.

Still, he had enough men left to man three trucks and fill up their cargo compartments with just less than a platoon. Already he had been on radio. Already he had alerted mechanized forces, tanks and units with armored personnel carriers. His aviation unit officers wanted to argue about launching reconnaissance craft and helicopters at night in low visibility during the bad weather. Markocevik wasn't hearing any arguments.

Besides the original battalion that had been ordered into action even as he was driving toward the killing site, a brigade was on the way, both in the air and on the ground. They would cordon off this part of the forest and wait for armored units to arrive in the morning. By midday tomorrow, he would have an entire division in the field squeezing the land like a sponge until there was no room left for the Americans to hide.

He knew well that they were Americans. The French had traded NATO planning documents and U.S. PER-LOBE technology for first rights to market his new liquor. Markocevik had held out for a big buy of French passive radar equipment that could be modified to receive PERLOBE signals and triangulate the transmitters. He had personally engineered the interface between radar and gun-firing directional equipment. He had insisted that a PERLOBE signal could become a firing target in under two minutes. Ironic that. The superb system that he had put into place had nearly killed him on the road away from the massacre site.

He had been forced to leave without that videotape. Now he was eager to get back. He would not wait for any other units. Would not allow that videotape to remain even in Serb hands. With something as dreadfully important as that tape, the only person in the world he could trust was himself.

BY THE TIME Swayne and the others had traveled half a mile, the artillery fire had been shut off. But new sounds in the distance worried him even more. The throbbing drone of helicopters. Many helicopters. He could guess the sequence of Serbian orders. They had detected radio transmissions and PERLOBE signals. A platoon or more had swept through the woods to investigate, with a larger force put on standby. The firefight. The discovery of Petr. The growing suspicion that the enemy presence was more than a guerrilla force moving around in the woods. Now the reserve forces were being launched to this hot spot.

So much for the invisible mission, staying out of sight and sound of the enemy.

Swayne had kept to a straight heading, one that he had set on his GPS. He had purposely set the course to avoid going directly at the squad-size engagement he had last heard. He would try to bypass the enemy by half a kilometer to the south. Then he would turn square and travel another half a kilometer. He would continue until he had traveled around the battle site, hoping that Night Runner would intercept them so they could get out of country without having a run-in with the airmobile force. Finally, he would head for Macedonia, due south.

It was a good plan, he thought. Except for two flaws, both of them fatal. One, they were not going to get out of Kosovo before the American bombing began. Even if they took up a direct heading and started out of country right away, they might not make it. Two, he knew of three, possibly even four enemy forces in the area. Running into any one of them was going to throw a gorilla wrench into his calculations.

Besides, even if they made their circuit without being engaged by Serbs, nothing guaranteed that they would run into Night Runner. Nothing—

Swayne dropped his knees at the sound of a hiss. He threw up his night-vision binoculars in the direction of the sound and found Perfect.

Perfect pounded the air with his right fist as if knocking on a door. In his left hand he had his golden retriever by the collar, fighting the straining dog, whose tail whirled, whose ears were alert and square.

Swayne knew the signal well enough. They had rehearsed it often enough. The dog had hit upon a scent of death. Either fresh blood or bloated bodies. Possibly even long-dead victims of a mass killing. In shallow graves.

That made it official. The third fatal flaw. The unknown contingency. Swayne began working the possibilities through his mind as he worked his way toward Perfect.

Zavello had already called off Event Scenario 16. They were not supposed to be looking for the dead bodies anymore. But the dog might not be alerting on dead bodies. It could be the blood of somebody wounded. Possibly Night Runner. Orders were one thing. Leaving a wounded member of the team—he would not allow himself to consider that Night Runner might be dead—was inconceivable.

He heard shouts of Serbs no more than a hundred meters away in the forest. He heard the drone of helicopter engines grow louder. He heard the echo of Zavello's command to get out of country.

When he reached Perfect's side, he took the dog's

neck in the crook of his arm and held him so Perfect could pick up his rifle.

"Any idea what he's alerting on?"

"Fresh blood," said Perfect without hesitation.

Swayne did not doubt the kid for even a second. He had watched the pair perform as a team during training. He had seen the dog pass by grave sites in which butchered animals had been left to rot, giving them no more than a cursory sniff. He had been astonished that the golden retriever could be led through a course a kilometer long with live caged rabbits and pheasants, quail, chickens, kittens, and even female dogs in heat. Going for the object of its existence, a spot where cadavers were buried or where human blood from the hospital's plasma bank had been spilled.

It was as if Gus had given up his own animal instincts simply to accept the training that Perfect and the Marine Corps had demanded of him.

So when Perfect said Gus was alerting on blood, Swayne knew that blood it was.

He felt like asking if it was Night Runner's. But that was ridiculous. And as it almost always did in a combat situation, Swayne's well-laid plan took a major turn.

Gus might not be able to communicate whether it was American blood somewhere upwind. But he could lead the team there. And Swayne could find out for himself.

He had to know. Yet he did not want to know. But he would. He gave his men a quick briefing, reminding them of known enemy forces in the forest, calling their attention to the sound of helicopters, which meant there would soon be more.

"We have to move quickly, find Night Runner, then get our butts out of the woods," he said. "Everybody understand?"

Two murmurs were all the answer he needed.

He gave a nod, and could see Perfect's perfect teeth

glint in the starlight. The kid was eager to show his stuff. A good Marine, thought Swayne.

The dog in the lead, Perfect followed. Then Friel. Swayne tried to keep his mind on the tactical situation, but it was difficult. All he could think was: At the end of that scent trail there had better not be the body of an American Indian warrior.

Orders be damned. There weren't enough Serbs in Kosovo to pay the price for the loss of Night Runner.

NIGHT RUNNER PROWLED the forest like a cougar, moving quickly in short, stealthy dashes, then stopping in place to put his senses to work on picking up his enemy.

It wasn't hard. Men with weapons who stayed close together could be awfully brave, especially when the object of their ambush had not fired back a single shot. They had let up on firing into the forest again. This time they did not hear a sound. They would not have expected to hear a sound anyway. At least not from behind them, the direction from which Night Runner stalked.

Somebody gave a command—he could tell from the tone of the voice, although he did not understand the language. Night Runner could see three men within ten meters. All three laid their rifles on the ground or propped them against a tree to dig into their combat packs or to fumble with straps on their webbing.

He knew what they were doing. It made him smile to think how well they had chosen a move that would cover him. He put away the Iraqi sword and took the dagger from his boot.

All their attention had turned to their combat gear. They felt sure they had killed him—setting their rifles aside proved that. Their next step was a matter of overkill. And as they focused on taking frag grenades from the spot where each man liked to secure them, he could as much as stroll up to his first kill. As he moved, knees carried high, setting down each foot toe-first on the outside of the boot, rolling the foot flat without crushing vegetation, never landing with a heel, he pulled one of his own grenades from an inside jacket pocket. He did not even feel the cuts he had gotten from crawling over flint earlier.

His were Space Age concussion grenades called boomers. Each sphere, cut in half, was hinged so a soldier could carry the boomer with the flat side against his body. They were light enough so one man could pack half a dozen, the total weighing less than three conventional grenades. The explosive was light. The casing was aluminum. The blast was lethal, not because of fragments that it threw, but because of the concussion. So wide was its killing radius that the boomer was too dangerous for a man with a weak arm to throw.

Night Runner closed the two halves together, and magnets both held them in place and activated the timing and detonation devices.

By touching two buttons at once, he armed the boomer, leaving it set on its default timing of 3.0 seconds. His right thumb kept one button depressed. When he threw it, releasing that button, the timer would start. He cocked his right arm behind his head and pointed his left hand in the direction from which he had heard sounds of men, including the commander of this squad.

When that man hollered his signal for everybody in the Serb squad to toss their frags, Night Runner went into motion.

He heaved his grenade, and on the follow-through stepped up to the soldier who had thrown his frag and crouched in the forest to pick up his rifle.

The man's grip never closed on the Soviet-made AK-47 assault rifle. Because a powerful left arm closed like pliers on his neck. The soldier tore at the elbow, but only for a second as the tip of a combat dagger plunged into his abdomen. The blade entered at the wishbone where his bottom ribs came together at the sternum.

The Blackfeet warrior, who was trained in the anatomy of death in a way that his people on the Plains could never have been trained, jerked the hilt of the knife laterally. The keen, black blade cut through the vital organs, severing pulmonary arteries and slicing into the chambers of the heart. More important, it cut a six-inch gash through the peritoneum, the sheet of muscle that separated the chest cavity from the abdomen. Tightening that muscle was what caused air to be drawn into the lungs. Cutting it left the man breathless. Literally. He could not breathe. He could not force air to call out.

So Night Runner dropped him, letting him fall where he might, and moved to the second man, who lay on the ground covering his head, unable to hear, unwilling to keep his eyes open to be blinded by the blast of his own grenade.

He would never open his eyes again. Because the tip of Night Runner's bayonet slid into the space between the back of his skull and the top of his neck, severing the spinal cord, cutting to the center of the brain. Night Runner cocked his wrist to the right, moving the blade to the left, and withdrew it on a line different from the entry wound.

Two killings in two seconds. Night Runner dove at the third man, also lying outstretched. He landed on the man's back. The man protested, probably cursing him in his language. Night Runner buried his face in the man's neck as the succession of grenades went off, half a dozen small explosions followed by one slapping, snapping, powerful blast that shook the forest floor and knocked branches and leaves from trees. The instant it was over, he was up and running, leaving a third man's throat cut.

He did not stop to pick up rifles, although he liked the AK-47 and was well trained in shooting it.

The AK-47 was a white man's weapon. And he was not a white man at this moment.

He found four more men, all dead, within the killing

zone of his boomer. He checked pulses to be sure they would not come out of a stupor and catch him off guard.

Two more men lay moaning on the ground. One had lost an arm to a flying tree branch. The other, covered in leaves and twigs blown from the forest canopy, lay with the muzzle of his AK-47 sticking out of his back. He had rested it against a tree, from the look of things, and the boomer had flung it through his body.

Night Runner figured two or three more men to go. He heard one voice call out, a plea for help. He crouched in the underbrush, hiding as well as he could, considering so much foliage had been stripped from the bushes. A second voice told the first to be quiet, by the tone of it. And a third voice reprimanded the second. Night Runner recognized that one. The commander of this squad.

Two men left who could be a threat to him. Two men who knew he was in the forest stalking them. Smart enough to know that the boomer was not one of their own explosions. Looking for a movement, waiting for a sound. Probably ready to open up even on one of their own. Two frightened men, armed to the eyes, and one wounded Serb. Hardly a fair fight, thought Night Runner, as he prepared to finish them off.

THE SOUND OF Night Runner's boomer among those of the conventional frag grenades brought Swayne to a halt. He knew Perfect would look back toward him through his night-vision scope, so he held up a hand to indicate a stop. When he saw Perfect crouch, he showed the hand to Friel, too.

As usual, Swayne's mind processed combat information like a Cray computer. Dozens of factors went into the mix that he mulled over in his head and evaluated by his gut before making a decision.

The brief firefight told him many things. First and most important, Night Runner was alive. Somehow he had gotten himself into a hand-grenade battle with his enemy. That didn't add up, but it did not mean there was a problem. Any fight of that kind Night Runner would win. Not only because he had the superior weapon—one boomer could do more damage than a dozen frags—but also because he was Night Runner. What's more, not since the first two instances of shooting did Swayne hear any gunfire. What he did hear was from the AK-47, which made a hefty bang compared to their own M-16 ammunition. Night Runner had both video and starlight technology and could have taken out a squad simply by shooting and moving, shooting and moving. Yet Swayne had not heard a single M-16 report from the BRAT light machine gun. It meant one of two things. Either Night Runner had lost his weapon, which didn't seem likely. Or he had set it aside in favor of one of his blades, his favorite weapons because it made him feel like one of his ancestors to fight like one of them.

Swayne could also guess that the squad had radios. If the leader believed he was in contact with an enemy force, he would report it. The platoon that Swayne's group had already slipped away from would change course and begin marching toward the new battle. The helicopter force might find a place to land nearby and maneuver on the spot as well.

Swayne took out his handheld computer and brought up a screen with a topographic map on it. He adjusted the light so the LED would show features in red and preserve his night vision. He cycled through various options on the high-tech maps, isolating spots that were level for at least a hundred meters, which would allow plenty of landing clearance for a dozen helicopters. Then he brought up an overlay of foliage, and eliminated any area that was not both large enough and free enough of vegetation. Two sites. One a mile away to the north. Another half a mile away to the east.

A special feature of his latest computer program could also give march difficulty for any type of travel. He isolated the spot where the grenade battle had taken place, and drew a line from it to both landing areas. He instructed the program to calculate the march difficulty for a company-size formation of soldiers on foot.

Even before the computer calculated the result, he read the token graphic lines and knew what it would tell him. The nearest landing zone presented the most difficulties, with a steep ridge to climb and a deep ravine, with a stream in the bottom, to cross. The approach from the east was over relatively level ground and through open forest. And it included a series of trails. Unless the Serbs were idiots and could not read terrain on their own maps, they would land and approach from the east.

The platoon would approach from the west, Swayne decided. So he and the team would move eastward. Night Runner, when he disengaged from his squad contact, would move south, away from the other enemy forces. They could easily link up if everybody marched according to Swayne's calculations. He almost laughed out loud at that. As long as he had been in this business, almost nobody played according to his rules, sometimes not even the very men he commanded.

Swayne checked his GPS and pointed his arm, giving the course correction. He flashed a hand signal to Perfect: a closed fist, then four fingers, a closed fist, then five fingers—045 degrees, due east.

He waited, but Perfect did not move out. He checked through his night-vision binoculars, and caught the tail end of a signal of Perfect's own. He saw enough to know that his man was trying to talk him out of the change in direction. The fist, two fingers, the fist again, seven fingers—027 degrees—east-northeast.

Swayne felt his temper flare like a gas flame suddenly turned to high. Night Runner going Stone Age on him. Friel being Friel, always in the gray area of near-insubordination. And now Perfect trying to tell him he would rather go off in a direction of his own, which meant that he wanted a Force Recon Team to follow the dog instead of the orders of its leader.

Swayne stood up and marched at Perfect as if they were on the parade ground instead of in the combat zone.

He got in Perfect's face, as much in anger as to keep his voice from carrying.

"What's with you, Marine? When I give a command in a tactical situation, I'm not used to having people question it. Not any people. Do you think we have time for a discussion and a democratic vote every time I want this team to do something?"

Perfect snapped to attention. Swayne almost laughed. It seemed so ridiculous here in the forest. Still, you did your second-guessing in the debriefing room over cups of coffee, not under the stress of a field mission.

"Did you understand my course change?"

"Yes, sir. Zero-four-five degrees, sir," murmured Perfect, his voice trembling.

"Move out then," Swayne growled.

"Sir, yes, sir." Perfect started to throw up a salute, but caught himself. Force Recon Team did not identify its officers under combat situations by saluting them. He whirled and brought up his arm to shoulder level, pointing out the course for his dog. The golden retriever glanced in the direction of the wind, the direction he had wanted to go, but with less hesitation than his handler took up the course change.

Swayne checked the animal's direction of travel with his GPS and shook his head as Perfect stepped out. He was right on course.

FRIEL WATCHED EVERYTHING through his own night-vision sniper scope, a smile playing at his lips. On past missions he had been the goat. Anytime the captain or Potts or even Night Runner had wanted to rag on somebody, he was their man. Nice of Perfect to come along

and pick up some of the slack, take on a few of the ass-
chewings. But when the captain grabbed Perfect by the
collar and jerked him back, Friel laughed outright. Was
the captain going to do more than chew ass on the freaking new guy? Was he going to kick his ass instead?

SWAYNE PULLED PERFECT back and pushed him up
against a tree.

"Sir, I did what you told me—"

"Quiet." Swayne brought up his rifle and trained it on
the dog.

"Captain, don't shoot my—"

Swayne slapped him across the chest. "Don't be an
idiot, Perfect. Shut up. Watch the dog."

The golden retriever had frozen in place, its ears
perked, squaring the large head, making it seem even
larger. Then the animal lowered its body to the ground.

The two men took their cue from Gus. They knelt,
too.

Swayne whispered, "Do you hear anything?"

"No, sir, just helicopters in the distance. To the east."

Swayne wished that Night Runner was with them. His
hearing would have been equal to that of the dog's. Or
at least superior to their own. Maybe he could have
sorted the audible signals well enough to tell them what
lurked out there in front of the dog.

Swayne put his mind to work on the new situation.
Something was out there. It could be near. It could be
in the distance. The dog had no way of telling them. If
it was an enemy force, Swayne wasn't about to march
straight at it. His options cycled through his head.

He could not take the course correction to the right
hand, possibly into an unknown danger. To the left
would be the squad that Night Runner had engaged, possibly soon to be reinforced by a platoon. Swayne would
not backtrack—that would take him away from Night
Runner. He cursed to himself. The damned forest was

getting downright crowded, turning into a regular circus.

The best chance for picking up Night Runner and moving out again as a unit, clear of this area and out of Kosovo, was to return to the course that Perfect had suggested when he delayed following Swayne's orders. Swayne swallowed his pride and gave a new heading, the direction closer to that Perfect had wanted to follow.

"Zero-two-zero."

"Sir?"

"You heard me. Get moving north-northeast."

As they crept through the forest, Swayne felt less concerned about acting like an idiot than finding Night Runner.

NIGHT RUNNER REALIZED he had lost much of his edge. Although he could identify just three men left who might do him damage, they knew they were being stalked now. They knew that somebody had sneaked into their midst. They understood how dangerous he was because they knew now they had lost most of the squad.

The man whose voice he now knew to be the leader's had called out, his tone demanding a report. Only one other man had answered, the one who had already spoken up before. A third soldier had simply shrieked, indicating he needed help. After that, Night Runner heard only muttering. The squad leader was reporting his plight over the radio.

Night Runner calculated his options.

He could withdraw, having killed most of his enemy. But that was no real option. That would mean he'd have to admit to himself that he had not even tried to recover his rifle with the incriminating videotape, which was his rationale for disobeying orders in the first place.

He could use another boomer, now that he had pinpointed the position of survivors. Using the concussion grenade did not require a second thought when he knew he was up against perhaps a dozen men. Now there were only two.

In the distance he heard the sound of helicopters, and just ten meters away he heard two men talking again. They might be discussing their own rescue, if they could just get those helicopters to land and send out the cavalry. Even as he thought about what they might be thinking, he heard the change in pitch of helicopter blades as the craft began to descend. They were going to land— that was the worst-case scenario, so he had to consider it. They were going to land to the east of his position, possibly within a mile of the spot. He didn't have much time left to dispense with these two.

Night Runner put together a quick plan of action. He slithered to his left until he found exactly the situation he wanted, grateful for the new leaves on the ground that absorbed the sound of his movement. He selected a tree about six inches in diameter. He lay down behind it and sighted toward the two men, who knelt back-to-back, each looking left and right in fear of where the next attack might come from. Too bad he had not taken an AK-47 off one of the dead after all. One burst would finish them both.

He looked upward, checking the tree's crown to see that it was large enough, and checking that the tree was tall enough to do what he needed it to do.

He checked behind himself. Twenty meters away stood an enormous hardwood too large for two men to link arms around.

He took a pair of boomers from his jacket, applied some custom settings to the explosives, and fastened them to the trunk of the tree on the side of the two Serbs. He used Friel's bad-ass duct tape, grateful that the stuff was so strong, but even more grateful that it could be unstrapped without the ripping noise of normal duct tape.

Next he found a flat stone and taped it on top of the

grenades so the stone pressed the explosive devices against the tree.

Then, feeling for the digital start buttons, he set off both timers at once and bolted for the larger tree. He ran full speed, not caring so much about making noise. In fact, hoping to create enough sound so both men would face in his direction. He didn't worry so much that they would get off clean shots. It would take a second or two for them to adjust positions even enough to fire blindly.

He was more concerned that the grenades might go off before he got behind cover.

For he had positioned the stone so it would help create a directional explosion, shearing the tree. He pictured how it would happen, the base of the tree kicking his way, the top staying in position, then toppling silently, then crashing through the forest to the ground.

The Serbs had heard him. He heard both of them shout. He heard the sounds of them fumbling and stumbling to lay their rifles in his direction. He heard a curse as one rifle apparently did not fire. The snap of the safety being taken off. A burst of gunfire splattering the trees above his head.

None of that mattered as long as he—

—he ducked behind the hardwood in time.

An instant before both concussion grenades went off.

Night Runner had crouched, welding his back against the rough bark, pressing the palms of his hands against his ears, protecting his eyes by pushing his face to his knees. Still, the blast of two grenades hit him from both sides with enough force that he thought he might have been caught in a head-on collision.

He had no time to indulge himself with self-pity over how much it hurt.

He dashed to his left, knowing both men, even if they had survived the concussion and the bits of rock blasted their way like grapeshot, would have been blinded by the flash. Even so, he would take no chances. He would not risk that an injured man would continue firing his gun in the last direction it had been pointed.

He heard the crackling of the tree falling in the forest, shrieking as it ground against the other timber, falling in the direction of his enemy. Now, he knew, they would not be interested at all in him, but in their own safety, worried about being crushed like characters in a cartoon.

After he had cleared himself laterally by fifteen or twenty meters, Night Runner turned and ran back on a line parallel to the fallen tree. He didn't worry too much about making noise. Both men had been close enough to the blast to be deafened by now.

He found the tree. He listened, but could not hear any sounds coming from beneath the branches, which had fallen on the spot where the two men had huddled.

So he worked his arm through the branches, checked two pulses, found two dead men. One had his face sand-blasted off. The other might have as well, but Night Runner could not move him from beneath the tree branch that had practically cut him in two.

He checked for weapons. The second one he found was his own. Also smashed by the tree, bent just behind the breech.

That did not matter so much. He might not be able to fire the weapon, but he had recovered the image of the massacre preserved on miniature CD-ROM disk in the gun camera.

He had also recovered his self-image. From some-where Heavy Runner had watched him this night. Had, in fact, watched over him. Heavy Runner would be pleased. Night Runner would never tell the details of his departure from the mission. Nobody would ask the right questions. And he would not volunteer anything. It was enough for him and Heavy Runner to know.

From the very second he had redeemed himself, Night Runner's mind began to work on matters of the military, rather than his coming to grips with his heritage. Where was Swayne? Where was Team Midnight?

All at once the reality of his Marine Corps existence hit him. Helicopters had landed, maybe two kilometers away. In his blind radio call, Zavello had warned the team to get out of country before American bombers began strikes—he checked his watch—in just a little less than half an hour.

He checked his GPS to find the location of the rally point. Of course, it was impossible for them to get out of country before the strikes began. But the odds of getting hit seemed small. Unless he stayed where he was now standing, in an area where explosions and enemy activities would almost certainly be picked up by satellite surveillance. And where the first strikes would likely be targeted.

He put away his GPS, and had taken his first step on the way toward getting out of Kosovo when a man with a rifle jumped out in front of him.

Night Runner froze. The wounded man. The one who had been crying for help. He had recovered enough to get to his feet. And now he pointed his AK-47 at the center of Night Runner's body mass. Night Runner was as good as dead. Silently, he cursed himself for being so careless as to drop out of the character of a Blackfeet brave and into his white man's role. To have thought about escaping the country when he should have skulked from the kill zone of the battle.

The gun swung away, its barrel clattering off a tree. The man stumbled forward blindly. In fact he *was* blind, Runner realized, his face drenched in his own blood. Probably deaf, too. And senseless from injuries the boomer had caused.

Night Runner pulled his bayonet, its blade still sticky from the blood of other Serbs he had killed this night.

The man was just a meter away. One wrenching thrust upward below the sternum. One slash across his throat. One jab into the eye and a hook of the wrist as the blade was withdrawn. All ways to kill a man instantly.

The Serb lurched toward him.

Night Runner stood aside. The man came abreast, just inches away. One stab to the temple. One sweeping hook, a killing blow beneath the left kidney to sever the renal artery.

The Serb stumbled past. One poke at the juncture of skull and neck, and he would drop like a stunned horse at the slaughterhouse. And that didn't even take into account what Night Runner could do with his Bedouin sword.

A dozen ways to kill the man occurred to Night Runner, the warrior who wished he could have lived in another time to be a warrior among warriors. But two dozen reasons to spare the man won out, mainly that the Serb was no longer a threat, no longer an enemy. He was just a man. One that would be scarred for life, if he got through this night alive.

So Night Runner crept away so that neither man would have to kill the other.

THE FOREST—0437 HOURS LOCAL

BEFORE THE GOLDEN retriever had led the team more than a quarter mile, Swayne began thinking that they wouldn't have to follow the animal. All that was necessary was to face directly into the breeze and keep walking.

Another quarter mile and all they had to do was follow their noses. This creature with its superior sense of smell might be able to find year-old graves. But Swayne didn't need a superbly trained dog to trail the scent of fresh blood.

After another hundred meters, the dog stopped in place. Swayne moved forward. He found Perfect trying to urge Gus into a small clearing surrounded by the forest. The dog would not move.

Swayne put a hand on Perfect's shoulder.

"I'm sorry, sir," Perfect whispered. "I've never seen him act this way before. One second he's on a hot scent and the next moment, boom, he won't take another step."

Behind them Friel made the sound of a hamburger thrown on a hot grill. Swayne recognized it as curse words being forced through his teeth.

"Henry, you have something to say?" he said.

"Nothing to say, Cap."

Swayne waited for the inevitable smart remark.

"Nothing except I'm getting sick to my stomach. Can't you smell it, Perfect?"

"Smell what?"

Swayne recognized the odor all too well. Friel snorted, obviously trying to clear his nostrils of the fragrance of opened bodies.

"Permission to move crosswind and set up security," Friel said.

"Move out then," Swayne murmured, trying not to breathe deeply.

Perfect didn't get it. He had not been in combat before. For that matter, thought Swayne, neither had Perfect's dog. Having been trained on splashes of blood and buried carcasses and cadavers, the animal had never been to a true battle zone, which could never be duplicated in a field training exercise.

For himself, Swayne had been to too many. He lifted his night-vision binoculars to his eyes, knowing what he would find, knowing that the magnitude of what he would find was going to explain why the golden retriever felt unsure of itself.

A chill ran through Swayne. Not twenty meters away stacks of bodies lay in the clearing draped over each other, arms and legs woven into a tangle. The sight tried to mesmerize him, but he would not allow it. He switched his binoculars to infrared so he could pick up thermal images, and forced himself to look away from the dead, trying to find evidence of the living, Serb soldiers left here as security. Or a burial detail. He checked all around the edge of the clearing, looking into the forest to see whether any living bodies lay in wait for them.

He heard a groan escape Perfect's throat, and knew that the new guy had found the heap of corpses in the night-vision sight of his own rifle. Gus responded to his master with a tiny whine.

His stomach flighty and his jaws cramping, Swayne turned on the video recording device inside his binoculars to capture the evidence of massacre. He was both sick and angry. Yes, he had seen death before. Much too much for any one lifetime. In fact, he had caused too much carnage personally. Those things he had always been able to justify. The mission. Casualties of combat. The realization that he had gone into many situations where the people he had killed were seriously trying to kill him. But this was slaughter. Murder.

As he magnified images through the zoom lens, he saw the hands tied, the necks strung together. These men—many of them boys—had been killed indecently, with less respect than pigs.

An acid rose up in his throat, a hot, seething hatred for the beasts who would kill like this. He felt driven to killing the killers. He wished that the responsible people would come back here so that he could add to the pile of dead.

Well, they had been sent into this godforsaken, godless country to find evidence of mass killings. It was a mission that he did not want to succeed at. But now he had that evidence. At last Swayne knew that he would be taking back the hideous pictures that the leader of the Free World wanted. They would be shown to tribunals. But they would not be made public. Too gruesome. Besides, there was no way to establish that Kosovars had not committed the murders. No way to prove that these were not Serbs killed by the rebels. He considered all the arguments and counter-arguments that he would have to listen to in the high-level debriefing.

He was stalling. He did not want to do what he had to do next. Swayne summoned all his energy and tightened his gut muscles. Then he turned the infrared scope back on. The pile of bodies glowed, some places warmer than others. The heat signatures told him that most of these bodies were still warm. Freshly killed. In some of the gunfire that he had listened to from as near as a mile away.

Worse yet, a few arms and legs practically glowed green. The wounded. They were not dead yet, but were wishing they were dead, lying among the bleeding bodies. Wanting to escape a warm flow of blood from their comrades. Not wanting to be chilled in the rain.

The next part of the job had to be done, and Swayne lacked the courage to order either of his men to do it.

He stood up. He started to take a deep breath to brace himself, but the stench caught in his throat and forced him to cough.

He moved sideways, following the path that Friel had taken, until he had cleared the downwind stream of air.

"Captain?" The voice came from a stand of bushes beside him.

"Yes, Henry?"

"You have to go?"

"Yes."

"Want me to go with you?" By the tone, Friel did not want to. Who would?

"No. Cover me."

"Yes, sir."

"Don't watch me. Don't gawk—"

Friel picked up the chant: "Don't gawk, don't talk, don't walk, don't lock onto the obvious."

They had developed that in their post-mission training program after the foray into Iraq. Like Secret Service agents, who never dared pay attention to the object of their security, but focused their attention on the crowds and possible ambush positions, Swayne wanted his team to look outward. In the desert he had almost made a fatal mistake of staring too long at a campfire that his enemy had built for him to look at. That he had fallen for the ruse for only a few seconds made a strong impression on him. So they had trained for just such an occasion as this.

Swayne's job was to go into the middle of all the carnage in the clearing. His men had been trained to keep a close watch on the area around such a site as Swayne tried to get proof that the Serbs were killers. He was to find somebody alive in that mass of damaged bodies. They each had learned a few phrases in the language of the Kosovars—the obvious things like:

What is your name? Your age? Your village? Your nationality?

And a few more phrases critical to investigating war crimes:

Show me the place where people were killed.
How did this happen?
Who killed these people?

And finally, a question for people whose wounds would indicate they had been tortured:

Who did this to you?

He was to record the answers of people the team talked to. Interpreters would translate. It was all a part of gathering evidence, small pieces of the puzzle that could be put together to form a larger picture, a body of evidence that would someday be used to convict criminals in the court of international public opinion, if not in an actual war-crimes trial. Swayne could not have guessed he would have the opportunity to ask one of those questions of people lying wounded in a heap of dead bodies. He could never have guessed that he would be collecting a dying declaration in a killing field.

Keeping his binoculars trained on the killing zone, looking for the brightest, warmest of those bodies in his infrared scope, Swayne stepped out of the forest. His boots felt as if they were made of lead. His stomach began to clench. He was glad that his men were under orders not to watch him. He would not want them to see him throw up.

FRIEL HAD NO problem averting his eyes. In the early days of his time in Force Recon, he would return from a mission and go home on furlough. Back on the block in Boston, it took every bit of the little self-discipline he had to keep his mouth shut about where he had been and the things he had seen. As the numbers of missions began to rack up, Friel would go home and visit family. He avoided friends because he thought they had nothing in common with him. Besides, he no longer wanted to talk about the things he had seen and done. After the last mission, he had gone home almost as if it were a mission to sneak into a foreign country. He had seen things. He had done things. The Mooks he had grown up with had no clue. He could never tell them. Not because he was under strict security rules. But because they would never understand.

Not that it mattered. He would never go home again. Not after this night. If the family want to see him, they could come visit. Maybe meet him halfway. He just couldn't go back. Not after this. He wouldn't want any of his old gang to look into his eyes and see how he had changed.

PERFECT KNEW THE drill. But he could not take his eyes off the spot where all those people lay. He realized how lucky he was to be new to this team. They would not trust him to go out onto that bloody, muddy ground to ask these men who had killed them.

He realized something else, too. There was no glamour to this business after all. There was no glory. He began to think about medals and the stories he had planned to tell back home in the bars. The stories he would write like some Ernest-freakin-Heming-freakin-way of the new millennium. He doubted that he could tell the stories. Because he did not even want to know them.

NIGHT RUNNER CROSSED Swayne's trail about a kilometer from where he estimated all those people had been killed. He did not actually see the trail. He smelled the sweet, musty odor of a wet dog, and knew that the golden retriever had passed by. The smell of the man was still in the air, not as strong, but still there. And difficult to pick up over the earthy fragrance of blood and guts.

He took a moment to get his bearings and evaluate the situation. A check of his GPS confirmed his location. He moved in a small, quick circle of about ten meters, cutting the team's trail two times, making sure that he knew their course. A check of his watch established that they were within minutes of the NATO bombing mission that Zavello had warned them about in his broadcast. No way would they get out of the country before bombs fell. He knew he should hurry and join up with the team, though. With all the concentrations of troops in this area, there was a good chance that they would be targeted. Who knows how many missiles would be fired their way from airborne cruise-missile platforms?

That thought put him into motion, moving as quickly as he could without making noise. Bad enough that enemy soldiers might be lurking in the woods ready to fire at any noise. Perfect was still an unknown quantity. Night Runner wanted to die as a warrior. He would not ever surrender to another armed force as Heavy Runner had done in trusting the cavalry. But even worse would be getting shot by one of his own men.

He had not moved a hundred meters before he heard the noise that quickened his pulse and his footsteps. No time to worry about slinking through the woods now. He began to jog, then to run.

THE RAIN HAD begun to let up, and an early-morning chill began to settle on Swayne's damp shoulders. Or was it just the cold weight of what he had to do? It hardly mattered. If he stood any longer at the edge of the forest, events would march on without him. As little control as he had on his life and those events, there might even be less. He checked his watch. The bombing was due to start in nineteen minutes. The Serbs had soldiers around the forest in every direction but one. For now they had left open the one escape route out of Kosovo. He had no time to waste thinking about the horror of what he had to do before that last window of opportunity closed.

So he stepped out of the forest and into the killing field. Muddy canals filled with water told him the path that trucks had taken. He walked between the parallel lines to the spot where they stopped. He could see the ground was chewed up where those vehicles had turned around. He saw the bloody mess. Fighting down his revulsion, Swayne lifted the binoculars and searched for the brightest thermal image. He found a man's neck and an ear visible in a stack of colder bodies.

Wading in, Swayne rolled and tugged at corpses, untangling dead people, trying not to step on them, trying to keep his feet and ankles free so he would not fall over and land among them. He turned on the video recorder with his right hand as he cradled the man's—no, it was a boy's—face in his left.

"Who did this to you?" he said, using one of his stock phrases.

The eyes came open, as if he were waking this child from a bad dream. The boy began to chatter at him, and from the tone of it, Swayne thought he was probably begging for mercy. Swayne's instinct was to grip the face and shout in the ear. But he did not. He stroked the boy's cheek, wiping away blood and mud dampened by the rain and the tears. Again he asked his question. The boy did not comprehend and began crying, trying to get away, still begging not to be killed.

From the sound of ragged breath escaping a hole in the side of the boy's throat, Swayne knew it was already too late.

Still, he repeated his question. Still, the child begged. Swayne realized he was not giving him the information he wanted or needed.

Swayne's stomach turned over once more. Here he was, trying to get information out of a kid who was about to die. No matter that he was doing it for a good reason. It seemed sick and twisted to him. He should be trying to give first aid, not get information.

He felt rather than heard somebody trying to call out just a few feet away, somebody lying beneath the bodies three-deep. Maybe there was a chance. Maybe he could literally uncover his witness. Dropping his binoculars, he pulled at bodies. He found that the boy was a key to the puzzle of untangling them. So he gently dragged the youngster to the side. The boy wanted to struggle, but apparently the gunshot wound had hit his spine. It was a wonder that he was able to breathe at all. And his breath did not come for long. Swayne felt guilty that he had added extra stress, perhaps killing the kid earlier than he might otherwise have died. Then again, Swayne thought, it was probably a blessing to die rather than live any longer in this corner of hell.

Gasping, trying not to breathe at all even as his labor required him to breathe more often, Swayne pulled bodies aside and found somebody alive and coherent. An-

other man. He had heard the question Swayne had put
to the boy. He spoke out in his language. Swayne was
astonished that the man could stay so calm. He was asking Swayne a question. Maybe he wanted to know who
Swayne was. Maybe he was asking if he intended to
save his life or to end it.

Swayne put those speculations out of his head. He had
a job to do.

"Who did this to you?" He adjusted the binoculars.
The man's face filled the frame as he began to speak.

He had his voice and enough strength, and he did not
hesitate to answer the question.

Swayne could not take a chance. He asked the question again.

The man did not become impatient with him. He answered again. Swayne recognized bits and pieces of the
testimony as a repetition from before. He reached down,
when the man finished, to brush some trash from the
forest floor away from his face, or was it a piece of
someone else's gore?

Swayne touched a button on his binoculars, and the
field of view opened wider to show the full context of
this victim lying on his back, drops of water from the
forest canopy spattering his face, dead bodies burying
him. The man struggled, and Swayne decided he had
enough evidence already. He reached into the mountain
of dead people and moved more corpses off his witness.
He kept thinking, kept hoping that he would find a mir-
acle. That this man could escape. He would be a better
witness if he were alive to testify to the validity of the
videotape that Swayne had already taken.

The man's arm came free, and Swayne hooked a finger between the rope and the victim's neck. It had been
so rough and tied so tightly around his throat that it had
left him with a raw, bleeding collar of skin. Swayne slid
a folding survival knife out of its sheath on the leg of
his trousers. As Swayne worked a second finger between

the rope and neck so he could guide his knife blade
without killing the man, he was glad for the darkness.
The water that filled his eyes was not from the rain.

The last strand of the rope parted, and the collar fell
away. The man took deep breaths as if it was the first
time he was able to breathe in days. He muttered a word
that could only mean *Thank you*.

Swayne put the binoculars back to his eyes so he
could see how to help the man get free, so he could
determine whether he would be capable of being taken
out of this place.

Even as his hole in the pile of dead continued to grow,
Swayne realized he was wanting more than just to save
a life. He needed more than a witness. He had to redeem
himself for his part in killing Petr by leaving him lie
helpless on the forest floor—was it just an hour or two
ago?

If he could save this man, could he save his own soul?
Did men even have souls? How could they, after what
he had seen?

Finally he had unstacked the bodies and created a crater in the landscape of humanity. The man tried to sit
up, but was too weak. Swayne touched him on the shoulder and told him to stay down, his touch and tone more
assuring than the words the Kosovar could not understand. First he patted down the man's body in the dark,
seeking injuries with his fingers. No wounds or broken
bones that he could feel. Then he gently undid the buttons to check his torso. He found two bullet wounds on
the man's chest. One on each side, each a long tear
in the skin, one that grazed a rib. But neither had entered
the chest cavity. Somebody sweeping a machine gun
quickly across a line of living men had created almost
exactly enough space to miss this one man. He had lost
blood. Swayne hoped he was not too weak to travel.

Swayne took hope and felt a sudden surge of urgency.

He might save this man's life after all—if he could walk. He went over the body, arms and legs again, with both his hands. This time he clenched harder, trying to find a wound, willing to make the man flinch if he could find another place where he had been shot. The survivor of the mass killing put up with it as if he were inside Swayne's head, as if he understood completely that if he passed this cursory exam, he would be given a chance at life.

Swayne found another set of ropes around the man's ankles, hobbling him to keep him from running away from his death.

His hands trembling, Swayne cut the loop off each ankle. Then he found the man's hands and pulled him up to a sitting position.

The man gave him another thank-you.

"Are you all right?" Swayne asked in English, not knowing this phrase in the other's language. He hoped that the tone of his question would do its job for him.

The softness of the man's answer and a gentle pat on his cheek told him what he needed to know.

Swayne put one arm over his shoulder and cradled his witness behind the back, holding him beneath one wound. As he lifted, he realized how skinny the man was. First he had been starved, then he had been shot.

Swayne took a step. The man took a step. He was weak. Perhaps too weak. This was not going to work. They would never escape Kosovo trying to drag—

The man spoke to him. Swayne's heart stopped.

The man was telling him something. Swayne recognized one word. The man was telling him his name.

"Petr."

Swayne's blood chilled. The victim's name was Petr? Could it be?

"Petr?" he said, his voice trembling.

In the darkness he could see the man's head nodding. "Petr."

This was, indeed, redemption. Swayne was being given the opportunity to save Petr's life after all. And he would. No matter how weak he was.

Swayne shifted his feet, bent his knees, and swept the man easily off his feet.

The binoculars dug into Swayne's chest bone. His rifle, slung awkwardly over his chest, bounced against the back of his head. The ropes and bodies tried to trip him. It did not matter to Swayne. He was not leaving Kosovo without this man. This man Petr.

One more step and he would be free.

One more step and—

Swayne felt a hand close on his ankle. He almost leaped away, so horrid had this living nightmare become. The hand of the dead, reaching out of its grave of bodies, clutching at him, pulling at him, asking for mercy, needing help, trying to be saved.

Swayne pulled away. He could not save everybody. He had Petr, and Petr was all he needed to save. For now, anyway. Later on, he would worry about rescuing the rest of himself from this nightmare.

He stepped away from the bodies in the clearing, stepped toward the forest.

Walking away from the dead was one thing. Walking away from living people was another. It had to be done. He had to get Petr out of this country. He had to get him before the team of interrogators. He had to—

"Jack. Save me."

Swayne froze. Nina! It could not be, but it was. Her voice. Unmistakable.

He went through half a dozen explanations having to do with delusions and hallucinations. Half a second later he decided this was impossible.

Yet she spoke to him again. "Jack. Jack Swayne. It's me. Nina. Save me."

The man in his arms murmured a question.

"It can't be," Swayne answered.

Petr spoke to him. He spoke softly, calmly. Swayne did not know his words. But he understood his intention. Petr was telling him that he wanted down. He was telling him that he'd heard the voice, too. He was saying that as much as he wanted to survive, Swayne should not leave the woman behind.

Swayne, already under the influence of a night of terror such as he had never known, put down his man, and Friel materialized out of the darkness.

"Give a hand up here, buster," Friel said to the man. Then he turned to Swayne. "We have to move, Captain. This road has got trucks on it. I hear them coming. Maybe they know we're here. Maybe they want to bury the bodies. But they're coming."

"Jack?" The voice had weakened.

Friel uttered a curse. "I feel like we've been put in one of them bad movies about ghosts and shit. Captain, get us out of here," he pleaded as he put an arm around Petr and led him into the forest.

Swayne turned back and lifted his binoculars to the spot where he had felt a hand on his ankle. He recognized the hand. Saw it and recognized the long fingers, the slim wrist, the short nails that Nina clipped because she could not stand to type or to dial a push-button telephone when they were too long.

"Nina?" Although he knew the hand, he did not expect her to respond to his daydream, the dream, the nightmare, the hallucination—whatever it was.

"Jack? Is it really you?"

He knelt and began pulling at bodies again. Once in a lifetime was too much. Twice in one night had brought his nerves to the breaking point. He knew he could not be seeing these torn and bloody corpses. It was too dark. But as his hands closed on open wounds, and he pulled people from the pile once more, it was as if his fingers were transmitting visual images into his head. He did see them. And he did feel a sudden warmth as his fingers closed on a shoulder. A slight shoulder. That of a woman.

He put up his binoculars. He found her face. Reaching out, he swept strings of her hair free, and he saw her staring wide-eyed at him.

It was Nina. Of course. She was, after all, a television correspondent. He had seen her on two previous missions where his job had overlapped hers. He had saved her life on one mission in Iraq.

He checked out her body with the binoculars, but could not trust what he saw. All the wet places could well be blood, but that did not tell him anything. There was too much of it to be her own. So he took inventory of her with his hands.

She groaned when he put his hands around her waist. He probed, and found a bullet hole in her abdomen. His mind put together the pictures of human anatomy, and he tried to manipulate those images so he could decide that this was not a fatal wound.

But he could not know by looking through the binoculars just how serious it was.

"Nina, I have to roll you over."

She grunted in pain, but the sound meant that she was giving him permission.

He pulled on her body until she lay on her side. He lifted her jacket—the one she called her Dan Rather jacket. The wound he found, oozing a steady, pulsing flow, did not encourage him.

"I feel weak. I'm going to pass out. Jack—"

"Quiet, Nina. This is going to hurt. I'm going to lift you up."

"No, Jack—"

"Dammit, Nina, don't be stupid. And don't be stubborn. I'm getting you out of here. The Serbs are coming back."

She hit him in the face. Not with her hand, but with some object.

"I'm sorry, Jack. I didn't mean to."

"It's all right."

"Jack, Jack."

"Don't try to talk." He shifted his body so that he could lift her up. The sounds of the trucks were becoming louder.

"Leave me, Jack. I'm not going to make it."

"Don't be stupid, Nina."

"Take the tape," she murmured, straining the words through her clenched teeth.

"What?"

"Here." She handed him the object that had accidentally struck him in the face. "It's a videotape. It has this massacre on it."

"I already have taped—"

"Damn you, Jack Swayne. Listen to me. This is a live video of the killings. It shows the face of my killer."

Her words struck him like hammers in the chest. The evidence he wanted. The face of the killer. Everything on tape. He could do more than redeem himself. His team could redeem the slaughtered people in this clearing and many more like them.

But what struck him so hard was her giving in to death so easily.

She was pushing at him with the videotape. He took it from her hand and put it into his jacket, packing it away in an inside pocket.

"Leave me," she whispered.

"No way in hell."

"Then get me out of here."

That was all he needed to hear. He picked her up quickly and began to run toward the forest. Once he stumbled and nearly fell on her. Only by dropping to his knees did he save himself from crushing her body beneath his, perhaps making the wound worse. As it was, she groaned at him from somewhere deep inside her unconsciousness. Then he was up and moving away as quickly as he could, wanting to get away from that pile of bodies before he heard another voice calling to him for salvation. He doubted he could ever go back to face the task of unpiling corpses again. He would not go back into the hell he had seen in that meadow.

As it turned out, Swayne did not have to go back to hell. Hell came to him.

It began with a single gunshot.

At the sound of it, Swayne threw himself against the tree and moved around its trunk so that he and Nina would be on the opposite side of where the rifle had fired. Half a dozen things then happened at once.

Nina cried out in agony. Swayne saw Friel throw Petr to the ground. Petr cried out in pain, but as a Kosovar, he knew what was up. He crawled behind a pair of trees and lay flat, his hands over his head.

Perfect called out, "Attack. Got an attack over here."

"Stop shooting, you idiot."

Swayne recognized the voice. Night Runner! Night Runner was back. It was as if an archangel had been sent from heaven, the angelic cavalry to rescue them.

Swayne's joy was short-lived. Overhead, an artillery round burst. But it was not the type that rained shrapnel and concussion down on them. It was a parachute flare that lit up the forest. As the parachute carried the white phosphorus torch across the sky, shadows on the ground turned around their anchor points like a time-lapse movie of a thousand sundials.

Swayne saw an eerie shadow leaping from tree to tree in the forest. He also saw Perfect trying to line up his target. It was as if he did not understand English. Did not recognize the voice of his sergeant.

Swayne called to him. "Perfect, hold your fire. It's Gunny Night Runner."

Perfect still did not hear. He shot into the forest again, hitting the tree where Night Runner's shadow was rather than where the Blackfeet warrior had already been.

Swayne and Friel both knew that the flare meant trouble. Already their night vision was wiped out. Already their advantage of being able to creep around in the dark and escape detection was gone. Somebody knew they were here. Somebody was directing troops. It might have been the convoy, at least three diesel engines roaring, that now seemed certain to burst into the area at any instant. Or it might have been one of those units that Swayne had seen on the ground earlier. Or perhaps the helicopter unit, now dismounted, moving its way toward them.

But none of that mattered. One of his own men was trying to kill their best Marine. Maybe the best Marine in the Corps.

Swayne reached Perfect at the same time as Friel. He threw a hand beneath the barrel of Perfect's rifle just as he fired again. Friel dug into Perfect like a fighter who had his man cornered. Uppercut after uppercut he threw into Perfect's ribs. Just seconds later an arm went around Perfect's neck and a knife blade pushed against his skin, bringing a trickle of blood.

"Night Runner," said Swayne. "Don't kill him."

"No, let me," said Friel.

"Henry! Knock it off." Swayne put a hand on a shoulder of both Night Runner and Friel. "It was a mistake. An honest mistake. Let's get out of here."

They both let go of Perfect at the same time, and he sank to his knees. "I'm sorry, Captain."

Swayne heard a second whine, and realized that the golden retriever was confused by all this conflict and upset.

Swayne also knew what a mess they were in. They had to gather their evidence, their victims, and themselves to get the hell out of this place, which was about to become a hot spot.

Swayne's mind was jogged back to its most analytical

state. The flare. It meant that the enemy did not want to lay down a barrage on them. It meant that they were more interested in something else.

Perhaps survivors. Maybe they had been forced to leave before they had finished their killing at this scene. Or maybe they were coming back with a second load of victims to finish off. Or a burial detail had been sent out to cover the evidence.

"The tape," said Nina from her state of unconsciousness.

Of course. The tape. Very possibly the Serbs were worried that the tape might be found. Leaving dead bodies was one thing. Leaving a videotape record of the killing—if that was what it was, and he doubted Nina would be wrong about that, then the killers could not afford to let it be taken out of the country.

But why did they leave it in the first place?

The question hung in the air. Before Swayne could formulate an answer to it, another shot shattered the stillness around him. The shot snapped by his head and went singing off a branch into the forest.

"Perfect, you bastard." Friel began turning on him, lowering his own rifle.

"Sir, it wasn't me this time."

"Serbs," Night Runner said. "I see them. Coming from the southwest."

"You brought them on us like stink on shit." Friel spat the words at Perfect.

Swayne did not need to look to confirm what Night Runner told him. If Night Runner said it, it was so.

Even as he thought it, it became so, with other shooters opening up on the meadow. Swayne pointed and hollered directions. There was no longer any point in trying to be sneaky about it. He caught Perfect by the shirt as he ran by.

"Captain—"

"Never mind about that, Perfect. Pick up this woman

and take her with you. Be careful with her."

"Yes, sir."

"Henry—" Swayne saw that Friel had already taken charge of Petr, had already draped an arm over one shoulder and lifted the man's feet off the ground as he carried him into the forest, away from the gunfire that had already picked up in volume.

Swayne traded glances with Night Runner, and they both lifted up their rifles. Swayne saw that Night Runner's was an AK-47. He supposed that Night Runner had lost his in the earlier combat. It did not matter now. It only mattered that they begin shooting to cover the escape of the other two.

As they faced the volume of gunfire, Swayne picked the center and memorized the position of the muzzle blasts. As he did so, his mind was working on the possibilities. To judge from the direction, this was the platoon that he had seen coming up the hillside earlier—the platoon that had killed their guide, the first Petr.

He opened fire a heartbeat after Night Runner. They both worked over the enemy firing positions, according to standard procedures that they had long ago developed. Swayne worked from the center out to the left. Night Runner, so he would not overlap Swayne's fields of fire and waste ammunition, worked from the center out toward the right. By the time they had finished firing short bursts in one sweep, several cries came out of the night less than forty meters away.

In response to their firing, the enemy force opened up with everything.

But by then, both Night Runner and Swayne had shifted positions, sliding back away from the trees, seeking low areas, moving laterally to get away from the positions that they had given away by shooting.

"Boomers out," Night Runner shouted. His warning was followed by two grunts.

Swayne crouched, clapping his hands over his ears,

pressing his face into the ground so that his eyes would not be hit by flying debris. The boomers would blind their enemy if it did not kill them. He bunched his muscles, waiting.

One blast stung his body. He dug in and waited for the second explosion. When it came, Swayne jumped up and began running to his left. He stopped at the edge of the clearing and turned back. Several of the Serbs had not been hit. They resumed firing at where he and Night Runner had been, betraying their own positions once more. Swayne took careful aim and fired four quick bursts into those spots. Two cries came up. Night Runner, by now far off to the right flank, had begun firing as well.

The initial shooting had confirmed to Swayne that they were facing at least a platoon. Now the shooting was more random than anything, much of the gunfire directed upward into the trees.

Blind, injured, frightened men. Men keeping their heads down. Men sticking their muzzles out and shooting fearfully. The intensity of their fire diminished to a fraction of what it was.

Quite possibly they had been well trained in maneuvering in the forest. But they seemed to have little fire discipline now. Swayne took up a third position farther to the left flank. He identified two more targets and silenced the guns there. Then he turned and began running wider. The move took him toward the clearing, and he changed direction quickly. He ran toward the spot where he had seen his men, Friel carrying Petr, Perfect lugging Nina. Far to his left he saw Night Runner's shadow darting among the trees on a converging course. A random shot sounded behind him, but he doubted that it was aimed fire.

Once more he saw the pile of bodies in the clearing, and made a wide detour, hoping he would never see them again. He reached the safety of the forest and put a tree to his back. He called out as loud as he could, "Turn on your radios." It did not matter anymore that the enemy could pinpoint them. Soldiers on the ground were reporting their position over the radio by now anyhow. Better that they have communications.

Night Runner came up first. "This is Two."

"This is Spartan Four," called Perfect. His voice was strained. Out of breath from carrying Nina. And, no doubt, from shame for having tried to kill Night Runner.

Friel came on gasping. "Three, over."

"Give me a report." Zavello. He had been quiet for a long time. He surely wasn't going to interfere now. "When you can."

"Keep down the radio transmissions," Swayne said. He directed Friel and Perfect to hold positions as he and Night Runner caught up. It didn't take long. The two of them had extra baggage and did not even have enough time to catch their breath before Night Runner and Swayne found them. Night Runner bent at the waist and took Nina over his shoulder. She cried out in protest, but weakly. Night Runner took Petr's arm and weight off Friel.

"Cover us," Swayne said. Friel had already dropped to the ground and pointed his rifle back toward the clearing. Perfect followed suit.

Swayne gave them a course and moved out to the oblique from their original direction of travel. He would circle right. He did not want to waste any more time running deeper into Kosovo. He simply wanted to get to the border at the nearest point. From now on it was going to be a race. He had no idea how they could win it, not with these extra bodies that they dragged along. But there was nothing to do but try.

More shadows swept across the forest. At first he thought another flare had been fired above them, one that he did not hear. But then he realized that these were lights on the ground. Truck lights.

The odor of diesels came at them, and he saw three trucks begin swinging into a horizontal line, illuminating the clearing with their brights.

They had not gone deep enough into the forest before stopping.

"We have to keep moving," said Swayne.

He gritted his teeth. He did not remember that Nina was so heavy. He had carried her before. Across the room in her apartment to her bedroom as she clung to his neck. Now she was limp and heavy, her arms slapping his upper legs with his every step. Now and then he had to stop and put his ear to her mouth to be sure she was still breathing.

He did not like the way things had worked out. It would have been better if he and Night Runner had split up. Night Runner should be working with Perfect, and Swayne could team up with Friel. As it was, the two junior Marines were paired. Until they could all catch their breaths, it would have to stay that way. A second flare went off overhead. Then a third.

He told himself that the Serbs were using the lights to search through the pile of corpses, giving the team some time to put distance between themselves and the Serbs.

Sure, the Serbs might also be illuminating the forest so they could conduct a search for the Marines. But Swayne didn't want to think about that. Things were serious enough as they were. Things probably couldn't get any worse.

He heard shouting to his left. Another force of Serbs. Possibly the troops that had been airlifted by helicopters. He shifted direction once more, feeling like a rat trapped in a maze, being forced into ever more narrow paths.

He touched his radio mike to leave it on voice-activated mode.

"Friel, Perfect, get going before you get cut off. Try

not to give away your position by shooting."

He heard Friel snicker. He was glad for the smart-aleck attitude. Things had grown all too serious. Meanwhile two more flares had lit up the forest, and now half a dozen illuminated the sky like daylight. All the shadows on the ground now moved more faintly and were multiplied by six. It was like some kind of light show exhibit. And it was also as if the Marines were moths traveling across an illuminated lamp shade.

Okay, he thought, so he had been wrong before. Now the situation had gotten as bad as it could get.

No. He ducked involuntarily as the air popped and crackled over his head. More gunfire. A force had opened up on them from the east. A large force from the sound of the foliage being thinned in the forest. Swayne was glad that they were shooting from such a long range. Apparently shooting at shadows flitting through the forest. Very few rounds managed to reach the team, for all the muzzle flashes he saw and gunshots he heard. Those bullets that did fly by buzzed like hornets. Meaning that they had struck branches and were flying randomly rather than aimed, tumbling through the air.

Not that a tumbling random bullet wouldn't kill.

Night Runner called to him, and Swayne saw that he had dropped into a dry streambed. Swayne put down Nina, jumped into the ditch, and pulled her onto his shoulders again. Then he moved out after Night Runner. Behind him, he heard Perfect tumble into the ditch, followed by Friel's sadistic laugh. Perfect cried out, and Swayne turned in time to see that Friel had stepped on him. Friel laughed again, and Perfect cursed him out. Swayne didn't mind. If it brought Perfect back to his senses and out of the panic that had made him shoot at Night Runner, then he might recover.

He turned back to follow Night Runner, and heard a voice in his mind correct him. No, Perfect wasn't going to make it. In combat you had to trust your companion. When that buddy tried to kill you, he put the most important relationship in the world—even more important than any marriage—into doubt. Combat buddies did not shoot at each other, even by accident. Worse, if they did shoot at each other by accident, they would come to their senses once somebody called out a warning. Perfect had not done that. He had kept trying to kill Night Runner.

Swayne couldn't have it. Wouldn't have it. Perfect would have to go into another career field in the Marine Corps.

Finally, despite the confusion, it looked as if they might evade the enemy. Swayne stopped and put a hand on Friel's chest. Friel groaned, but knew what had to be done. He took the weight of Nina onto his own shoulders and continued down the ditch without complaining.

That gave Swayne what he needed. Friel and Night Runner now had the two wounded under their control. Next time they traded off, Friel and Night Runner would provide cover for them. Perfect and Swayne would operate together from now on. Swayne didn't trust Perfect, of course. But knowing the man could not be trusted gave him all the reason he needed to be cautious.

"Perfect, stand by," he said.

Swayne took out two boomers. He set the timers for four minutes each. One he threw back along their trail. The other he rolled into the ditch where they had all dropped down from the forest floor. Then he reset two more of the devices. This time to two minutes. He waved Perfect ahead, and followed him down the trail, dropping off the boomers like bread crumbs in the fairy tale, taking a second to cover each with gravel.

He caught up to Perfect and took two more boomers from him. These he set to five minutes each and tossed them into the forest on each side of the ditch. Then he began following his men, now and then looking back to make sure he could cover them if any of the enemy showed up.

Eventually the Serbs would close in on the spot where the Spartans had last been seen. They would probably gather around momentarily to get organized. Somebody would find the Marines' footsteps in the ditch. When the first boomers went off, men would seek cover, perhaps even diving into the ditch. In any case the random explosions would throw their pursuit into more confusion, and for a good while.

Behind him, he heard shooting. A good sign. From the area in the meadow where the bodies had lain, more shooting. A bad sign. He forced down the bile. He had saved all the lives he could afford to save. The Serbs would be going through the pile of bodies killing anybody who had survived, probably shooting anybody who was warm.

Making even hell a worse place to live. Or die, as the case would be.

It hardly mattered now. The team could clear this area now, and enough enemy soldiers were scattered around to prevent the Serbs from shooting artillery on their own.

Swayne turned off his radio mike and called out to his men to shut off theirs, too. No need to direct the Serbs on the ground toward them.

For now he had no doubt that they would be trying to catch up. That tape. They would have to have the tape if it showed what Nina said it showed.

Swayne began to think they might have a chance of getting out of Kosovo.

Then Zavello's voice came on the air, startling them in their headsets: "Spartans, this is Eagle One, get your heads down before—"

The earth belched fire all around them. The ground seemed to buckle upward at them. Fortunately, they were men of instant reflexes, Marines used to hearing warnings and reacting to them without analyzing them, without asking why, without asking how. All of them had already begun to dive to the ground on the words "get your heads down." When the first blast hit, they were already groveling. After that it was a no-brainer. The violent shifting of the earth beneath their feet would have knocked them over anyhow. The walls of their streambed crumbled, knocking stones and chunks of earth down onto them. More blasts shook loose more earth, and Friel found himself climbing on top of the rubble before more rubble fell down on him. He realized he could not afford to be unconscious. Lying still for too long would end in his being buried.

"One good thing," Friel shouted. "At least we know it's zero five hundred."

Swayne realized that the bombings had not been all that close. He would have been glad for the help from the sky, if only it had been back toward the west. Instead it was off to the east and south, the directions they wanted to travel. If they had not been held up, if they had moved out ten minutes earlier, they would have been at ground zero.

Although the sounds had rumbled by, Swayne still whispered to his men, encouraging them forward. All around them the sounds of rifle fire snapped through the forest—no, he realized, it was trees falling from the blast. Branches broke and fell. The landscape he could see from the flashes of more distant explosions had become a tangle of giant splinters. This part of the forest had become nothing more than one deadfall after another.

Finally Swayne called a halt as his men stumbled, Friel cursing at the unsteadiness of his footing, especially as he tried to get help from Perfect to carry Nina.

"Keep going forward?" Swayne said into Night Runner's face.

"Not much choice, is there? I ran into a squad before

catching up to you. Where there's a squad, there's a full platoon."

"The platoon that shot at us back at the kill site?"

"No," said Night Runner. "Probably part of a second platoon. And where there's two platoons—" He let the rest of his sentence hang in the air.

Friel finished the thought. "There's a company."

Night Runner grunted.

"That doesn't even account for the force that landed by helicopter," said Swayne. "Maybe a company. Maybe reinforced."

"Plus the three trucks," said Night Runner. "No telling how many are in there."

"We should keep going," said Swayne. "Keep moving down this creek bed toward the explosions. All this deadfall won't affect us as much as it will them. Plus it will give us a hiding place during the day."

Night Runner looked at his watch. "We have an hour before daylight," he said. "And Captain?"

"Yes?"

"It *will* affect us. We have to carry these two."

"Why the hell did they have to start bombing us right—"

Zavello answered Swayne's question before he finished asking it.

"Spartans, this is Eagle. I have been trying to shut off the bombing, but it's coming from headquarters much higher than mine. You can't take a chance on answering, but try to keep moving to your designated rally point. The next round of strikes will be to your west, based on your last location."

Swayne felt sorry for Zavello. It was harder on him to be in the headquarters than it was in the field. Given a choice, he knew the colonel would rather be out here with them. Except for the fact that his eye patch kept him out of combat, Swayne was sure that he would have found a way to get around his high rank and age to be here. He would have made up some story about conducting in-field inspections to neutralize the argument that such a senior officer couldn't afford to be risked in small-unit actions. And he could have gotten his fifty-eight-year-old body into shape. But no lame excuse and no amount of physical conditioning could overcome being blind in one eye.

Swayne gave his pity a second thought. Hell with that, he decided. Having Zavello in the field would be one long, never-ending pain in the butt.

Truth be told, he allowed, he was glad the man was half-blind.

He checked his own watch. They were far enough away to be out of danger, but he told his men to brace themselves anyhow. "Get your heads down. I have boomers out. Any second now."

The concussion grenades went off within seconds of his warning. After the bombing the team had just been through, the boomers sounded like mere firecrackers to them. But from the screams of injured men, Swayne felt a bit of satisfaction that his ordnance had been more effective than the Air Force's.

He gave Night Runner the signal to move on, murmuring to the team that there would be other explosions.

As they moved out, he visualized in his mind's eye the Serbs scattering from the area of the first explosions. As they traveled deeper into the tangle and the subsequent grenades went off, he could hear other screams in the aftermath.

He took a moment to get Perfect's grenades from him and set them to detonate in thirty minutes. It would probably take that long for the Serbs to get up the courage, reorganize, and follow them. If these last boomers did their job, the Serbs might be discouraged enough to back off altogether.

THE KILLING ZONE—0503 HOURS LOCAL

DURING THE BOMBING, men all around Markocevik dove for cover, but he was quick to see that the explosions were off to the north and west. From the size of the blasts, he could tell these were bombers. Somehow, NATO had finally gotten up the nerve to stop bluffing. He might have some men in the area, he realized. Sure enough, within seconds the radio was filled with reports of casualties. He did not care. As long as among those casualties were the Americans.

Even as flashes lit up the northern horizon, he called his officers and senior NCOs together. He gave orders to them to go through the pile of bodies, looking for the video camera that he had been forced to abandon when his own artillery had opened up on him.

After he had given his instructions, he realized his subordinates were staring at him.

"Do you have a problem?" he asked.

A young captain of infantry spoke up. "Are you serious, my general? You want us to go through this mass of dead? Why can't we bring up a detail of prisoners to—?"

The captain never finished his sentence. As he turned and swept his arms at the masses of the dead, Markocevik's arm came up. In his hand was a pistol. As soon as his arm was level, the muzzle of the pistol just inches from the man's ear, Markocevik pulled the trigger. The captain's knees buckled, and he dropped into a heap. Markocevik shot him twice more. The other junior leaders recoiled. Except for one senior sergeant, who stood with an astonished look on his face as he was splattered with blood and brains.

All of the leaders scurried away to organize their soldiers. All but the one covered in gore.

Markocevik shrugged and raised his pistol again. "The others do not doubt that I am serious, Sergeant. Do you?"

Markocevik had to step aside as the man fell toward him, a bullet that had passed through the captain's head lodged in his throat.

JUST MINUTES LATER, somebody shouted, and a non-commissioned officer retrieved the video recorder from one of his men.

Markocevik opened the recorder by smashing it against the bumper of one of his trucks. When the tray slid open, it revealed what he was most afraid of. Nothing. The tape was gone.

Another set of guttural commands sent his men scurrying back to the pile of bodies. At his orders every man was laid out on his stomach. A detail went down the rows of corpses, shooting each one in the back of the head to finish them as possible witnesses.

Finally, his aide-de-camp, a major, by now very nervous about being the bearer of bad news, brought him a section of rope. The loop used for the neck had been cut. Markocevik scowled. The major hesitated, but showed him another section of rope, this one the hobble that Swayne had cut off the male prisoner.

Markocevik cursed. He sent the detail to count bodies once more.

Nobody could say for certain how many Kosovars had been in the group executed. The Serbs had long ago set a policy that they would not make the same mistake as the Nazis in keeping detailed records of their executions and burials. One thing Markocevik could deduce, however, was the number of American civilians. The three members of the CNN television crew were accounted for. But there was no woman. Nina Chase had escaped. She had the tape.

He might be able to counter evidence stolen by some

special operations group, claiming that it was merely Kosovar propaganda. But when a newsperson had that tape, that tape with evidence of her own attempted execution on it—

He cursed long and violently.

The people around him shrank from him as he stormed back and forth in the headlights of the truck. Officers gave orders to men to begin a search of the area, more to get away from their commander than to find the missing woman and the videotape.

Finally he gave a command, and he seemed collected and determined in giving it.

"Find them," he said. "Find the Americans. Bring me that woman. Dead or alive. But I must have the tape. Whatever you do, I must have the tape."

He knew that fear alone would be a strong enough motivator for his men. But he decided to sweeten the deal, shouting an offer to any of them who brought back the tape. "One million dollars," he crowed. "One million dollars in United States currency to the man who brings me that tape."

Markocevik gave orders for that message to be communicated to the helicopter force that had landed to the north. He then directed that his trucks be sent back to the first military compound to pick up more soldiers. He ordered another division of tanks from an armored headquarters two hundred miles away to move—no matter how dangerous—and march toward the nearest border with Macedonia so that the Americans could not escape. He had to have that tape, and he would sacrifice his entire army to bombers if that was the price that had to be paid.

After that, he called defense headquarters and demanded that a company of helicopters be detailed to him. He would use them to scour the forest looking for signs of his enemy. Military headquarters wanted to ar-

gue with him, but not for long. He threatened to talk to
the president himself. Nobody dared to call his bluff.

THE STREAMBED—0532 HOURS LOCAL

SWAYNE AND HIS crew found the going slow as they
neared the area of ground zero. It wasn't necessarily true
that intelligence analysts wouldn't bomb the same sites,
but he hoped that they would choose other areas inside
Kosovo, find larger targets than six people stumbling
over and under fallen timbers.

He was grateful for this creek bed. Even though many
trees had fallen across it, Swayne and his crew were able
to wriggle their way underneath. After a break when he
could give water to everybody and take time for the team
to pound down some calories, Petr, one of his precious
living witnesses to the massacre, seemed stronger.

Nina did not. She drifted in and out of consciousness,
and Swayne wasn't able to help her very much. Night
Runner had spent a good deal of time packing bandages
into the exit wound in her back. He had used his anti-
septic powders liberally, although a good deal of dirt
had already gotten into the wounds.

Swayne thought of AIDS. For her blood had been
mingled with those of the dead men, almost certainly.

From the look on Night Runner's face, it wasn't going
to matter very much. He bandaged her waist as tightly
as he could, and Swayne noticed in the first dim light
of dawn that he avoided direct eye contact.

"Should we give her narcotics for the pain?" Swayne
asked.

Night Runner shrugged. "It wouldn't hurt. I don't
think she's going to be able to walk anyhow. Once we
get clear of this deadfall, we can make a litter and carry
her between us a lot more quickly."

He didn't say it with any conviction, and Swayne had

to fight off the brief sadness that tried to engulf him. This was no time to be grieving. He would do the best he could to get her out of here. He would save her life if he could. She was valuable. Not just to him because, he realized, he loved her. It was perhaps the first time he was able to admit this to himself. Of course, he had told her those words. In passion, he had thought. She had expressed her love for him, too. Neither one, though, was quite sure of the other, it seemed.

But now he was. He did not want this woman to die.

It was ironic, too. The Marine Corps and the United States would not now want her to die either. She would be a persuasive witness against her would-be killers. She would be proof positive of war crimes and atrocities. He tried to imagine Zavello telling his nemesis in the White House that a member of the media would be vital to the national interests. But he couldn't get his mind around the incongruity.

He patted his jacket, feeling the videotape underneath. Nina and Petr and this tape. Nobody who had given Team Midnight this mission could have dreamed that they would bring back something so indisputable.

The Serbs, if they knew this tape was missing, would be after it with a vengeance. If its contents were ever revealed to the world, United Nations forces might actually be shamed into taking action, might actually be prodded into a decisive military response.

He shook his head. Doubtful. Then again, if he did not get this tape out of the country, nobody would ever know. Nobody would ever be put on the spot to act either bravely or cowardly.

The others waited for him to tell them what to do. So he did, throwing out one hand to tell Night Runner to start moving. Petr no longer needed to be carried. Strengthened with the calorie-rich food of the Force Recon rations, he helped Friel pick up Nina and thread her limp body over and under the forest's deadfall.

Then, leaving behind two more boomers set on delay and thrown well out of the ditch, Swayne moved up with them. Once the Serbs had been burned a few times by following their trail directly, they would spread out into the forest. He hoped that they would be walking by this spot in an hour, flanking the dry creek bed, when those boomers went off.

The team reached a spot close to the line of bomb craters. Here it was not a landscape as much as a moon-scape. The blown-down trees and gray earth looked like the slopes near Mount St. Helens after the mountain erupted.

Beneath the deepest tangle, Night Runner turned and took Nina's weight off the shoulders of the man carrying her. Perfect slumped against a pile of soft, newly turned earth.

Friel surprised Swayne by telling Perfect, "We don't have time for a blow in place. I'll take security up ahead. Perfect, get you and the dog you rode in on out there on our back trail."

Perfect had hardly spoken since he'd shot at Night Runner back at the massacre site. Swayne wasn't concerned about the kid's feelings. All he wanted now was for him to perform. Swayne wasn't so much worried, now that the sun had come up, that Perfect would try to shoot any of his own again.

Night Runner briefed Swayne, saying they should stay in this spot while he took a quick look around the landscape to scout a safer spot outside the ravine.

"It's not going to do us any good to stay in this creek bed," Night Runner told Swayne. "They don't have to search it. All they have to do is strafe it, maybe bomb every inch of it. Hell, all they would have to do is dump gasoline down its length and touch a match to it."

After Night Runner returned from his recon and briefed him once more, Swayne agreed to the Gunny's plan at once. He helped the others move north, following the path of the greatest resistance along the line of the bombers' flight that had created the devastation. And away from Macedonia. It was hard going, but he knew that ordinary people would expect them to be headed for the border. He doubted that anyone in the Serb Army would have the tracking capability of the Iraqi that had vexed them on the last mission.

Once he had put his team and the wounded into a hideout beneath a fortress of fallen tree trunks, Night Runner worked quickly back toward the spot where they had previously rested.

After the experience in Iraq, he had added a couple of lightweight items to his pack. One was a duster made of turkey feathers stitched together at the quills. It looked like part of a war bonnet, but when he rolled it tightly, the quills and their binding became a handle, and the feathers could be used to put the finishing touches on a track to make it vanish. Once that was done, it could be used like a fan to airbrush the other marks away. In all the dirt that had been moved and the fine dust that had settled down after the bombings, Night Runner could make the footprints go away, even if a platoon had walked along the path.

In this way he erased the trail of his team from the dry·creek bed. Once he arrived back at their current resting place, he was glad to see so many footsteps left by Friel and Perfect moving around to provide security and Swayne treating their wounded. These he did not erase. Instead, he created a false trail down the creek bed. It was an old trick, and one that he had used in Iraq with mixed success.

He returned to the creek bed by a fresh route. Moving by himself, he didn't worry about wiping out tracks. He could move without making them in the first place.

After he had gotten clear of the collateral damage from the bomb strike, Night Runner began running through the forest toward the border. He did not worry about leaving a false trail any longer. Once the Serbs decided on his direction of travel, all they would need was the occasional footprint or scuff mark on the forest floor to follow. So he left enough signs to give them what they needed. He crossed a stream, making a mental note of its depth, width, and direction. After going another quarter mile, he stopped in a clearing.

He checked its size and the wind direction. It would work. This could be made to look like a helicopter landing zone. It was another old trick, but he did not have to be as elaborate as he was before, in the desert. He broke some branches of saplings, trying to create the impression that a helicopter had landed to pick up the team. For good measure he climbed a small tree and lopped off its top, then roughened its cut edge as if it had been hit with a helicopter blade.

Finally, he took out a carton from his rations, swiped it across his face and dropped it where it could be found.

Then he doubled back on his trail, stepped into the stream, and worked his way down the current, the wind at his back for a kilometer or so. He maintained a counterclockwise circle beyond the landing area and took a roundabout way back to his team, coming in on them from the opposite side that he had left.

He felt confident he had done the best any man could.

He knew that no man would be able to track him through the water—unless the man was a North American Indian trained to do so—or a Bedouin. He doubted either would be in Kosovo. But for good measure he circled a couple of times and then took up a roundabout path toward the spot where he had left his team. Only one thing could defeat them now.

Tracking dogs might follow the trail left in the air and with no difficulty. But only if somebody suspected they had been tricked. If the dogs—and there were none to worry about yet—got up to speed and followed the track he had put down. If dogs did follow his scent to the clearing, the track would end. It would take a devious mind and a helluva dog to undo his ruse.

THE DEADFALL—1430 HOURS

ALL DURING THE day, as NATO bombings carpeted first one part of the country, then another, Swayne's confidence grew. This wasn't like the last mission in Iraq, where his enemy could concentrate forces in the open and come after them with no qualms. Every time a force revealed itself, either by radio traffic or heat signature of running engines, they were in danger of getting picked up by satellite and overflight surveillance. The Air Force apparently had ordnance to burn because the bombing never seemed to let up. Nothing like a few one-ton bombs to break the focus of an enemy force.

Not that he was able to concentrate very much on his own. On the one hand, Petr seemed to grow stronger by the minute. He owed a lot of his recovery to the rations the team had fed him all day long. In fact, Swayne had to tell him to slow down because he didn't want him sluggish when it came time to escape. He did not want to have to carry two people, especially one that felt as if he had doubled his weight in half a day. Petr's spirits rose as his energy level rose. He wanted to talk a lot, although nobody in the group understood him. Swayne detailed Perfect to record Petr's story, using the little-used daylight videotape function of his electronic binoculars. The tape had four hours of recording capability, and if the man had something to tell them that might be used in a war-crimes trial, Swayne wanted to capture it.

Nina, on the other hand, was his main concern. She had not regained consciousness. Sure, it might have been the narcotics, keeping her out of touch. Most likely the weakness came from her loss of blood.

Lots of blood. Swayne changed her bandages every couple of hours throughout the day. Each time they were soaked. Before long, Swayne had used up all the sterilized dressings in the team's supplies. Then he used some clean socks from each man in turn, rolling a ball of cotton-wool cloth tightly and pressing it into her wound, then strapping it to her body.

He checked her pulse often, too often for his own liking. Each time he found it, but it was always faint.

As always, his mind ran through the possible options. Leaving her in place might be best for her recovery—if they had the capability to give her a transfusion. Maybe they could call in a helicopter and move her a short distance to a possible landing zone. He weighed that. Zavello would never go for it. Unless Swayne was able to sell her as a witness in a war-crimes trial.

If they could move her to Macedonia, just seven or eight miles away, he could use the radio and have medics standing by. But he did not think she could survive being carried that far like a sack of potatoes.

Swayne had gone through every possible option, and had entertained a few impossible ones, including a fantasy or two, when he saw the golden retriever perk its ears.

"Any idea what it is?" he asked Perfect, although he was not sure anybody could know on such slim evidence.

Perfect shook his head. Then he reached into his pack and brought out one of the experimental devices that they were to test on this mission. They were the bat's ears that he and Night Runner both carried. They were built like headphones, except that the ear cups were open and concave, as if a satellite dish had been cut in half and placed on each side of the user's head. In normal field trials, Swayne had listened to normal conversation at more than a kilometer. He could distinguish voices, if not words, at twice that distance. Swayne hated the device because it picked up too many stray sounds. And, if he were listening in one direction, it shut out his ability to hear in any other direction.

Of course it had the capability to filter out natural sounds and selected man-made ones with a bit of fiddling with the control panel. But Swayne never was fond of such gadgets, especially when he had somebody with Night Runner's sensory capability.

He waited as Perfect got into position behind the dog and directed his bat's ears in the same direction as Gus.

PERFECT WAS GLAD for the opportunity to be doing something, however small, to contribute to the team. He knew he would have a long way to go before he could make up for the trouble he had already caused. *Shooting at one of his own! What a disgrace.*

Any notion that he had previously had about trying to bathe himself in glory had long since been erased by the shame he now felt. He knew good and well—Perfectly well—that this would be his last mission. He had lost it. He had let panic set in and then rule him. They would not trust him ever again.

He tried to rationalize that they had not trusted him in the first place, had not given him a fair chance to prove himself. It didn't wash. Even with himself. Nothing could erase the disgrace of shooting at one of his own. One time maybe. But twice?

At first he did not hear anything. He took it as another failure. They would not blame the high-tech equipment. They would blame him. They—

"Dogs," he said, even as the barking reached his ears. He refined the settings on his handset and turned his head, swiveling it like a radar array. "Men's voices, following the dogs."

• • •

SWAYNE AND NIGHT Runner looked at each other. Swayne then glanced at the wounded woman. He locked glances with Night Runner again and shook his head. She could possibly be moved. Or they could stand and fight. But not both. Unless—

"We could leave Petr here to watch over her," Swayne said. "Maybe intercept them and fight it out. Let them follow us. Lead them away." When he said the words aloud, it sounded like a lame plan, even to him—something out of a Saturday matinee.

Night Runner said, "I could go take a look. Get a better idea of what they're doing before we have to act."

"I hate letting you go," said Swayne, who remembered how it had been having Night Runner gone earlier on this mission. That had given him fits for half the night. He didn't want to do it again, but he couldn't see any useful alternative. "Who goes with you?"

Night Runner shrugged. "Your call, Boss."

Swayne checked Perfect's face. The man's eyes were pleading with him to go along with Night Runner. He wanted to redeem himself, erase the doubt that he had planted in his team members' minds.

Swayne gave it only the briefest of thoughts. Everybody deserved a chance at redemption. He knew that. But it was not the job of the Marine Corps or this Force Recon Team to let a man save face or reputation. He would never approve Night Runner's plan on that basis alone. But the plan did make sense, and it would be stupid of him to deny that just because Perfect might redeem himself besides.

He gave a quick nod, and Night Runner eased into the forest, Perfect following. With a hand signal, Perfect instructed the golden retriever to tag along. The dog stood still for a moment, as though he was insulted that he could not lead this mission, but finally he did as he was told, his tail drooped to show his lack of enthusiasm.

Swayne marveled at the dog's personality. He had seen plenty of men act insulted when given formal commands that they did not want to obey—Friel, for example. At least the animal didn't sass back, as Friel had.

NIGHT RUNNER MOVED swiftly. He wanted to cover as much ground as possible, as quickly as possible. If anything, the Serbs would have search parties out all over the forest. He did not want to run into anybody until he had gotten well clear of the hiding place for the others. Even at that, he didn't want to run into any patrols that could stop him from getting to those dogs. He hated himself for what he might have to do once they found the animals.

PERFECT TRIED TO do everything perfectly. He did not want to stumble, so he concentrated on his footing. Yet he did not want to let down his guard, so he tried to keep looking up and checking the perimeter. Since he was following Night Runner, he knew he was responsible for their six members, too. So now and then he turned a complete circle to watch that nobody was coming up behind them or cutting across their trail. This time he would not screw up.

Except that his heel caught a root once as he was turning. It held his boot like a vise, and he had to crumble to avoid twisting an ankle or a knee. He landed hard on his back. Rolling over, he got to his feet. Got to his feet hoping that Night Runner had missed it. But no, the Gunny was staring right into his eyes. He could not figure out this man that Friel called Chief. He could not tell whether he was being condemned for his clumsiness or was simply being ignored. Night Runner just looked at him, then turned away and moved off into the forest. In three steps, he had disappeared. When Perfect reached the tree that Night Runner had vanished behind, he saw nothing. He stopped, confused. He knew well enough that Night Runner would not have disappeared unless he wanted to.

He was struck by a moment of panic. Would the sergeant be playing a trick on him?

No. Of course not. Night Runner was not one to pull pranks. He had vanished from sight because he did not want to be seen.

Which meant that he did not want Perfect to be seen either. So Perfect let his knees buckle, and lowered himself into a crouch. He remembered that he was not entirely defenseless. He put on his bat's ears and swiveled his head back and forth. He was listening for Night Runner, but he heard the enemy.

He chided himself once more for thinking that the sergeant would play head games on him in a combat zone. And he congratulated himself for taking the proper action.

But what to do next? Stay put, he decided. Night Runner would tell him if he wanted him to do something. He turned his head from side to side, trying to pick up sounds of his comrade. Nothing. Then he focused in the direction of his enemy.

He heard the sounds of boots moving through the forest, men plodding along with no particular concern for tactical silence. Men talked to each other in the language of the Serbs. There was the clatter of metal and the swishing of branches against clothing.

He put his mind to work on counting based on what he could hear. They had given him the ultra-sensitive hearing of a dog in this device. They had trained him to add his own intuition.

He felt a touch at the center of his back and flinched.

Night Runner murmured into his ear, "How many, do you think?"

Perfect had to turn his head to see if the gunnery sergeant was joking. He was not. He actually trusted him to give him combat information?

"Six, maybe seven men."

NIGHT RUNNER NODDED. "Eight, actually. But nice job."

"How can you be sure?"

The left side of Night Runner's mouth pulled toward his ear. It was the closest Perfect had ever seen to a smile. "I see them. Look." He tossed his head.

Perfect turned his head in the direction that Night Runner had indicated and felt a little prickle of shame again. He had concentrated all his attention on one of his senses, his electronic ears. But he had not opened his eyes to see what was plainly visible.

Moving in and out of the trees below was a squad-minus. Eight men, just as Night Runner had said. He supposed they were a search party. Like other men he had known on other missions he had been on in training, these men were not taking their job too seriously. They were simply tripping through the forest in single file.

"Are they on your trail?" Perfect asked.

Night Runner shook his head slightly. "No, just out on a Sunday stroll. They won't get serious again until somebody shoots at them or until somebody sends a bomb down the chute at them."

Perfect understood. The Serbs had probably put out dozens of squads like this. If a single one of them came into contact with the Americans, they'd make some noise—either by radio calls or by shooting—and all the other squads would converge on the spot.

"We let them go?"

Night Runner nodded.

Perfect understood. With the direction they were traveling, the Serbs were no threat. Just a patrol. Probably one of many trying to prevent the Force Recon Team's escape to the border. Night Runner stretched out on the ground beside Perfect, resting his chin on his hands.

Perfect studied his superior NCO. His camouflage markings on his face, neck, and hands were a work of art. Not like any other Perfect had seen. It had taken a second for him to realize that this warrior had painted his face with deliberate care. He had noticed in training that the pattern never varied from day to day. It reminded him of the markings of the Indians in the movies—which, of course, except for not being in the movies, they were.

Night Runner told Perfect to focus his attention on the job instead of on his face. All it took was a flicker of his eyes in Perfect's direction.

After five minutes had passed, Night Runner asked, "Do you have a direction on those dogs? Maybe a distance? A count?"

Perfect swiveled his head all across the horizon, turning his body even to check their back trail. Finally he narrowed his search to one direction, nodded to pinpoint the noise, and pointed.

"Two dogs barking. I'm guessing one to two kilometers. It sounds farther, but I think they are in that little valley across the ridge."

Night Runner nodded. He had already come up with a similar result. He tugged on Perfect's arm, moving it slightly toward the left.

"I'm thinking pretty much the same thing, except that the direction might be off. You might be hearing a reflection of the sound coming off that cliff wall to the right."

Perfect turned his head to study this new situation. He shook his head in awe.

Night Runner nodded in awe, too. He was impressed that the bat's ears had given a member of the team sharp enough senses to rival his own, except for being fooled by the echo.

Night Runner told himself to get over being smug. He gauged by the direction and distance that the animals had passed the point at which he had backtracked from the fake helicopter landing zone and moved into the water. Now all that remained was for the Serbs to buy his fake helicopter LZ.

But he would not allow himself to let his tactical situation and the fate of his team depend on his enemy acting the way he needed to act for Night Runner's plan to be successful. He considered all the possibilities, borrowing from Swayne's method, and arrived at the worst possible conclusion, so he could choose the best possible course of action to counter it.

Worst-case, the Serbs would not believe the trick about the landing zone. Say everything went wrong, and the enemy were able to counter his every move. Where would he and Perfect have to be to counter-counter?

And if they bought his ruse, where would he have to be to know it?

He poked Perfect's shoulder and gave a signal that he should follow. Then he melted into the forest. He had to ask himself a third question: Why was he being so silent, when Perfect was tramping along behind him like an ox cart drawn by a team of thirteen?

MARKOCEVIK GOT THE radio call he'd been hoping for. The dogs that he had ordered into the forest were tracking his quarry. They had left the dry creek bed once it had taken them into the forest. They were racing for the border with Macedonia.

He shrugged at that. He had already directed an infantry force to take up a half-mile-long blocking position on the most likely pass leading out of Kosovo. Mechanized units had already moved out to link up with the shoulders of that force. More men would be landed by helicopter on the ridges and peaks to keep the Americans contained. Units from both flanks would line the forest. Once this section of the woods was cleared, he would direct the patrols to re-form into units and begin pressing into the trap where the Americans would be caught.

But not without its cost. The allied bombers had struck the moving units. To counter, Markocevik had dismounted the troops and kept them moving on foot on a forced-march pace. Other troops would be trucked into the area to conduct a huge sweep, pressing the Americans against his blocking force on the border. They would not escape. They could not escape now that he knew they had that tape. No price was too high to pay for getting that tape back.

One day the war would be over. Either because NATO had invaded his country—which he doubted— or because public opinion in the West had grown tired of a protracted conflict with no visible result in sight. What did Americans care about Muslims slaughtering Serbs and Serbs slaughtering Muslims? He would bring Serb uniforms to the killing site in the woods and dress the corpses as if they were his own soldiers. He would photograph the scene. The mass killing would become a Kosovar atrocity. Nobody would be able to unravel the claims and contradictions. He would hire lawyers. The best international lawyers, to create doubt, to generate fog.

In time, all would be forgotten. He needed to be thought of as a military commander who had been successful. Even a standoff with the Kosovars would be a success in economic terms. Eventually foreign aid from the NATO countries would rebuild his country. And he could take his business of exporting fine liquors out of the country and into restaurants worldwide. In the saloons across the globe, a few drinks of his exquisite fruity drink would keep the tensions down. It would lubricate the willingness of others to forgive him. He would base his operation in France, the country that gave him his start. In time, he would be known as his country's most beloved patriot.

Unless that videotape got out. How could he have been so foolish?

He would spend the life of every soldier in his country to get it back. He would get it back if it cost the life of his own mother. When the Americans were done for, no matter that it cost him a thousand—even ten thousand— lives to finish them, he would display their bodies to the international press. He would have his evidence of a ground invasion that would justify putting down the Kosovar rebellion.

He already had a story in place with selected journalists, even a television correspondent at CNN, a colleague of Nina Chase—who had not died in his planned execution. But who would die as soon as she could be found.

He heard a crackle of the radio, stomped out his cigarette, and went to his vehicle, where the tone of the man making the report did not sound encouraging.

The news came to him as a stake in the heart. Somehow, the Americans had landed a helicopter inside his country. Or so it seemed. For the trail disappeared at a clearing. He listened to the conclusions of his commanders on the spot even as he waved one hand in the air, telling his aide-de-camp to summon a helicopter for him.

When he was airborne, he caught himself composing a press release denying the charges of mass execution. He found himself saying that the film was a sham, a fake put together by technicians who could tell the most outrageous lies by editing digital images electronically.

His arguments sounded thin, even to himself. Even he would not accept such preposterous explanations.

No, the videotape would have to be found. And destroyed. Along with the woman and the Americans. Even if he had to send agents outside the country.

Once at the landing zone, he had his plan. It was a plan of desperation, to be sure. But at least it was a plan of action.

Before the blades on his helicopter had stopped rotating, he called his leadership together.

"Get the dogs over here. Let me talk to the handler."

Markocevik could read people, and he was glad to see that the dogs' master was young, energetic, and eager to please. He wanted to move up in the world. He was cocky. He would risk anything, sacrifice anything, even his animals. He knew this man would do what he wanted.

"Do you have proof that these invaders escaped on a helicopter?" he asked.

The men around him looked to each other for answers, each hoping somebody else would have the proof that Markocevik had demanded.

When he saw that nobody could confirm a helicopter flight on radar or a visual sighting of a craft in the air or the actual sound of a landing, his hopes rose a notch.

To the dog handler, he said, "There may be soldiers in these woods. I want your dogs to find them."

The handler stared at him.

"Get busy," said Markocevik.

"But my general—"

"Can your dogs find these men or not?"

The handler did not miss Markocevik's body language, his right hand going to the grips of the pistol at his waist. "But you have dozens of men in the forest—"

"Hundreds," Markocevik said. "So the loss of one incompetent man and two incompetent dogs will go unnoticed."

The handler spoke quickly. "Sir, with all respect, neither I nor the dogs know of any way to tell the difference between the men you want and your soldiers."

Markocevik narrowed his eyes and shook his head.

"I need an article of clothing," said the man. "If I can put the odor into the dogs' noses, they will follow it to the end of the earth."

"How did your dogs follow a trail to this spot?"

The handler spoke to a sergeant who had been in charge of the squad detailed to follow him. The sergeant held up a battered rifle stock and said, "We found this at the place where the . . . the battle took place last night, where the Kosovar rebels died. It has a scent on it—"

Markocevik pointed a finger at the sergeant's face.

The sergeant went right to the point: "The dogs took their scent from this rifle and followed it to this spot, where the track disappeared. And we found this along the way. With the same scent." He held up the ration packet that Night Runner had left.

Markocevik tore Nina's silk scarf from his neck, where he had worn it since the execution. He tossed it to the handler. "Take this. See if the dogs can pick up her trail anyplace around here."

The man took his dogs out of the mass confusion in the helicopter landing zone and waved the fragrance of the woman's scent at their noses, holding back their leashes as they went for it, telling them to find this odor. When he was sure they had identified what he wanted, he took them along the back trail insisting that they find it. They did not.

After only five minutes, he ran back to the spot where the helicopter was supposed to have taken off. Nervously, he started running the dogs in circles wider and wider.

Twenty minutes later, he trudged back to Markocevik.

"My dear general, I apologize. The dogs are unable to find this scent." The handler cringed, as if he expected to be shot on the spot. A look of surprise creased his face at Markocevik's reaction.

Markocevik grinned broadly, a smile of joy and triumph. The woman had not left the country on the helicopter after all.

"They are still here." He took the dog handler by both shoulders and shook him. "I assure you, my son, you have done nothing wrong. They have tricked your dogs by making a track that seemed to disappear where a helicopter landed. It is not so. They are somewhere here in the forest yet. In Kosovo. Now we must find them. Tell me, if you were trying to escape your dogs, what tricks might you use?"

The private beamed. This was a skill that he knew well. He understood things about his dogs and the fragrance of man in the air that others could not comprehend. He began to babble, explaining all he knew to Markocevik.

But Markocevik wasn't having any of it. He shook the man's shoulders harder. "If I ask you the time of day, do not tell me how to build a clock. I do not want to be taught your trade in dogs and tracking. Just tell me how a man played this trick on your animals."

The handler nodded earnestly. He knew something about false trails and hiding trails in water. It had been part of his dogs' training. He gave Markocevik the information he wanted, talking until the general showed him the palm of one hand.

Markocevik briefed his officers to set up and wait for more dogs to be brought in. He directed his aide-de-camp to stay on the ground and wait for another set of dog handlers to follow the track of the man who had lost his rifle stock.

Markocevik looked to the officer in command of all the troops around the clearing, troops standing idle. "What are you fools doing? Smoking your cigarettes? Joking around? This very moment somebody might have you in his rifle sights. At any time American bombers will unload their ordnance on this spot. You have no idea how many people would like to kill me and dismantle our country. If I die, you die."

That put the Serbs into motion, moving to the perimeter of the clearing, getting as far away from Markocevik as they could.

"And one other thing," he shouted after them. "If you

bring me that tape and the woman, you will be rewarded as I have said. But if you do not bring her to me, you will never leave this forest, alive or dead."

He had not actually said that he would kill anybody. But nobody in the forest who could hear him would doubt it. They had seen him in action before. They knew that killing was his ecstasy.

From high ground a kilometer away, Night Runner watched. Perfect had already told him the bat ears picked up the man speaking. He could make out the words, although he did not understand the language. Night Runner instructed him to record the conversation. Who knows when it might come in handy later on?

But he was more concerned about the actions in the clearing following the talk. He did not understand what was happening when the dogs did not go back to work a second time, trying to find him. Instead, the handler and the two animals were loaded onto the helicopter. He watched them take off and head back in the direction of the massacre site.

What did it mean? That they bought into his ruse? That they believed he and the team had escaped? That was an explanation. If the Serbs thought they had taken off in a helicopter, they would have no more use for the dogs and send them back to their kennels.

But why, then, were Serb soldiers forming a perimeter at the spot?

Borrowing Swayne's methods again, he tried to come up with a worst-case scenario. When it occurred to him, he didn't like it at first. Then, of course, he realized that he was not supposed to like thinking about the worst that could happen to the Spartans. He was the gunnery sergeant responsible for doing something so that the worst could not happen.

"Let's go," he said to Perfect. "We have to get back to the team."

•   •   •

SWAYNE HAD ALWAYS liked working under radio silence. It kept higher headquarters out of his head, for the most part. And if the command wanted to talk to him, they could do so, but he would not be expected to have to reply to them. On the other hand, when one of his men was separated from the team, he hated it. And right now he wanted to hear from Night Runner.

He needed to know what the Serbs were doing. He wanted to have a clear picture of the tactical situation so he could find a way to get Nina to a place were she might get medical attention.

At the thought of her, she whispered his name. He went to her side. He leaned close so she would not have to speak loud. As it was, she could barely make a whisper. He had to watch her lips, trying to read them.

Her mouth said, "I love you."

He was glad Friel could not hear. "Save your strength, Nina. You'll need it when we have to get you out of here."

"No," she mouthed.

"Yes."

He could not make out her next attempt at talking. Or maybe he did not want to understand that she was trying to tell him she would not make it out of the forest alive.

She was a different woman from the one he had known: vibrant, determined, defiant, professional, cocky, demanding. Her face now showed nothing but pain and weariness. He could not be sure—and did not want to think it—but it seemed as if she were on the verge of giving up. Once that happened, he knew, it would be over for her. With all the loss of blood—

"The tape," she whispered.

He patted his chest. "I have it. Safe and sound. Right here."

She made another sound he could not understand. He leaned in close until her mouth was at his ear. With a great effort, she began to talk to him.

When she had finished, Swayne sat up straight. He had never known Nina to be so concerned about things other than herself and her career in television. What she had revealed to him transcended anything he had ever known about her. He had liked her—make that loved her. He still did love her. So he was willing to overlook many of her faults, and there were many. Maybe he loved her because he and she had nothing more in common than that they were out of sync with the rest of the world in their own peculiar ways. Other than the Marine Corps as an institution, Swayne had nobody he respected. With the possible exception of Nina. For her part, besides him, almost nobody respected her. She would never have had the job she did if she were unable to find her way into impossible situations. Such as the one that had put her life in such grave danger. American television would always have a demand for somebody who could put herself on the receiving end of a mass murder.

As soon as Night Runner returned, Swayne could see that he was agitated.

He gave a brief report of what he had seen in the clearing and said, "We have to move in a hurry. Way I figure, they will try tracking us again. From the kill site. This time with dogs."

Swayne looked at Nina. He did not know how well she would be able to withstand being moved again. Especially if they had to hurry. If they had to move her at all, it would be best to be careful about it.

A thought struck him. There might be a way to get her and Petr out of the country along with the tape. He took the members of the team aside and briefed them on it, as Petr tended to Nina.

When he had finished, Friel continued shaking his head, as he had during most of the briefing.

"This would be the second bullshit mission in a row where I get to make like the Peace Corps," Friel said.

He tossed a nod at Perfect. "Send the freaking new guy."
He did not even try to hide his disdain.

"Knock it off, Henry," said Night Runner. "Do what
you're told."

Swayne had already considered sending Perfect to
take his two witnesses safely out of Kosovo. Petr had
continued to get stronger, and he could help carry Nina.
The dog would provide security. But he worried about
Perfect's lack of experience. And about that instance of
letting his panic take over. Swayne would rather have
Friel in a fighting situation, but he did not know whether
Perfect could—

"Captain Swayne," said Perfect. "I may not be able
to navigate as well as the Gunny, but I can follow a GPS
as well as the next Marine. Besides, Gus can help provide security. His ears are as good as—" he caught himself—"almost as good as the Gunny's."

Night Runner cleared his throat, and Swayne saw in
his eyes a silent recommendation.

"Okay, Marine, you can do it." Just to cover all the
bases, Swayne had Night Runner check the accuracy of
Perfect's GPS settings. Then he repeated his instructions.
"Take this heading," he said, tapping on the screen of
the GPS. "The Serbs expect us to cross the border here,
to the east. Go north instead." He pointed out the Kosovar stronghold that had been identified by intelligence
reports as late as yesterday before the action in the forest
had begun.

"Don't make any radio reports," Swayne said. "I don't
want the Serbs shooting any more artillery at you. We'll
hold them long enough for you to make this rally point."
He put his finger on the preprogrammed spot on Perfect's LED screen. "After we make contact with the
Serbs, they'll direct all their attention to us. It'll be safe
to send a helicopter to pick you up."

Finally he handed over the tape cassette. "Nothing
matters more than getting that video out of Kosovo. If

we fail, all those lives were wasted," said Swayne.
"Guard this with your life."

Swayne clapped Perfect on one shoulder, and Night
Runner grasped him by the other. "Good luck, kid," said
Night Runner.

"I won't let you down, sir, Gunny."

Swayne did not want to waste time, but he did take a
moment to whisper in Nina's ears while the rest of his
men turned away to give him privacy. She responded to
him, but weakly.

Swayne then did his best to brief Petr, telling him with
hand signals that he should help Perfect carry the injured
woman. He pointed out the direction they were to travel.
The man seemed to understand well enough, for he
started to pick up Nina right away. Swayne held him
back as Night Runner went to work fashioning a litter
from two poles and two ponchos in their packs.

After the three had set off, the dog in the lead, Night
Runner took the point, headed in the opposite direction.
Swayne fell in behind, and Friel brought up the rear. No
longer held back by the wounded and no longer bur-
dened by worry about Perfect, the trio practically ran
through the woods.

NIGHT RUNNER SET the course a good ways downwind
of their original track. If the Serbs were able to get moving faster than he expected, the team would be in a position to set up an ambush. And the bloodhounds could
not betray them. Night Runner hoped the team would
never again draw a mission that did not involve combat.
He realized that for months he had been in a state of
constant change. Change that would lead him away from
all the baggage that he carried from the white man's
world. Change that would take him closer to his heritage
as a Blackfeet warrior.

● ● ●

FRIEL COULD NOT get the smile off his face. To be rid of the weak was to be living large. First, the chick. Just by being a babe, she was weak. But as half-dead meat besides, she'd get everybody on the team an artillery enema.

The Kosovar couldn't speak English. So, by definition, he, too, was weak. Useless. Helpless. And, for all anybody knew, one of the Serbs anyhow. Perfect was both weak and stupid. He did not belong in this group of fighting men, and Friel was glad that he himself had been able to dodge the detail of leading the weak to safety. He snorted. Of the whole bunch, the dog was probably the most dependable, but no matter how you cut it, he was still a freaking dog.

To be shed of every last one of them? Things were definitely looking up.

SWAYNE HAD BRIEFED a simple plan. Perfect would get the witnesses and videotape out of the country. That would accomplish the Force Recon Team mission no matter what happened to him and his two most dependable Marines. They would get into position to prevent the Serbs from following Perfect's little band. He would do whatever was necessary to delay those following. Kill the tracking dogs. Ambush the enemy with hit-and-run tactics to keep the Serbs preoccupied. Maybe they could even draw the blocking forces away from the border, get them traveling in convoys on the roads, make them vulnerable to NATO tank-killers. He was not sure that he and his men could evade the Serbs indefinitely. Then again, they didn't have to. If they could keep the Serbs occupied long enough for Perfect to get that tape and those witnesses into the hands of NATO forces, they would have done what they were sent here to do.

Getting Night Runner, Friel, and himself out of Kosovo alive—that was another question altogether. Once he could be assured that the first part had been done, he could afford to spend some time planning their own escape. Engaging a division-size enemy force with three men. Keeping them occupied for hours. Drawing attention to themselves, including artillery strikes and possibly air strikes. And, of course, once the Serbs had begun to concentrate, drawing NATO bombs as well. *Be honest,* he told himself. *There's no point in wasting time even planning an escape.*

But as they jogged through the forest, Swayne began working out solutions to his problem. It took a huge effort trying to suppress the idea that it was stupid even to consider that he and his two men would survive. He ought to be saying his prayers instead of—

Whoa! A sudden idea hit him. He'd been worried about hitting the Serbs and running away. Maybe there was a choice between the impossibilities of trying to engage a whole army and trying to evade the same army on the lookout for him.

He had two dependable witnesses to a massacre— dependable because they were victims of the atrocity. On top of that, he had a videotape that documented the killings, and from what Nina had whispered in his ear, pictures of the killer giving orders.

After they had cleared the blow-down area of forest where bombs from NATO planes had been dropped, he decided. Only one thing could make this mission more of a success than getting the witnesses and tape out of country.

As long as they were taking on impossible missions anyhow, why not bring out the defendant himself?

Why not indeed?

Swayne pursed his lips and granted himself a lame smile. Then, since he was out of radio contact with HQ anyhow, he granted himself the change in mission.

EVENT SCENARIO 17

PERFECT TRAVELED WITH his rifle slung across his back. He carried the front end of the litter, moving carefully but quickly. Against his chest, the videotape felt hot. He knew what was on it. He understood its importance. At this moment, he was in charge of the very essence of the mission of the Force Recon Team. No, he *was* the mission. Swayne had given him a chance to prove himself. He didn't need to prove himself a hero, as he had once thought. He no longer wanted to prove himself a best-selling author. He just wanted to get that tape out and remain a member of this Force Recon Team. If he were successful, a heroic thing would have been accomplished. But he would not consider himself a hero. He just wanted to get a job done. Imagine. He was being given the most important part of the mission. And it did not even involve fighting the enemy directly. What a concept.

The first few times his golden retriever stopped and

alerted, he would put down the litter carefully and show
the palm of his hand to Petr, indicating he should stay
put. Then he would move forward to see if he could
hear or see what the dog had alerted on.

Gus never failed him. Each time Perfect was able to
put on his bat ears and find sounds that did not belong
in the forest. He kept his eyes open, too. The Gunny
would have been proud of him. Twice a patrol passed
by them, and once he saw a formation of tanks moving
into line at the base of a ridge a kilometer away. And
each time, he swung left keeping to the northerly direction of travel, eventually working his way back on a new
line toward his pickup point.

At first he had not trusted his captain. Left on his own,
he would have turned more directly north rather than
traveling a course that took him toward the enemy. But
as he could see the terrain unfold before him, he realized
that Swayne had given him a route that would take him
around sheer cliffs that he would never have been able
to navigate, even without carrying the wounded woman.

That captain. He had never known anybody who knew
so much, yet talked so little.

The fourth time that Perfect went forward on one of
Gus's alerts, leaving Petr and Nina behind, he saw a
squad of Serbs less than fifty meters away. At first he
thought that Gus had let him down, letting him get so
close. Then he realized that most of the men were lying
on the ground sleeping. A couple were drinking from
their canteens, and one man was going through the rem-
nants of a pile of rubbish, ration cans, and boxes. Perfect
realized the group had stopped to take a meal break.
Besides, the wind was not in the dog's favor, and the
men were keeping quiet. Perfect decided that he should
cut the dog some slack. Without Gus, he probably would
have blundered right into the open on the trail that ran
just above the squad.

Perfect checked both the ground and the topographical

map on his handheld computer screen. He was traveling along the base of a granite bluff. The trail led across a clearing. If they had tried to cross it, they would have been pinned against the base of the cliffs, sheer walls behind them and gravel scree below them. He saw that there was no way to avoid these men and no way to sneak by them. He realized he would have to wait them out. He worked his way carefully into the shelter behind a boulder and kept watch from his overlook. As he waited he could not keep his mind on the importance of his mission. It had grown heavier than the litter he had been carrying. Now, as he lay on his chest, his heart beat against the videotape cassette. Or was the videotape taking on a life of its own, its heart beating against his?

He thought out his options if that enemy squad were to awake and start coming up the hill toward him and the others. He realized there were no options, really. He would have to fight them alone. He checked his rifle. He would have the advantage of surprise. He could probably knock out four, maybe five of the Serbs before they got organized. Then it would be four or five of them left against him. Not good odds, even for a Force Recon Marine. Maybe he could get up and run away after killing some of them. But his mission included getting those two civilians out of Kosovo. Running away was not an option.

He felt ashamed even for thinking it.

He took the videocassette out of his jacket and stared at it. Everything depended on getting this tape out safely. But if they shot him, all they would have to do is pick up the tape, put a bullet in his head, and two more in the remaining heads in his group. End of story. Forget about glory.

He could not let that happen. He did not have enough confidence in himself to prevent it, though. He tried to comfort himself by asking: What would Swayne do?

What would Night Runner do? Much as he disliked him, what would Friel do?

He signalled his dog to his side. Scratching the animal behind the ears thoughtfully, he wondered, what would Gus do?

THE FOREST—1756 HOURS

SWAYNE CALLED A halt after Night Runner told him they were within a kilometer of last night's massacre. He gathered his two men into a tight perimeter in the underbrush. They sat facing each other in a compact triangle, each watching over someone else's shoulder so they could maintain all-around security. Swayne took out his handheld computer and brought up the pre-mission background menu. In short order he found what he wanted, loaded it onto the screen, and passed the computer around.

It was a picture and biographical summary of his target.

"Markocevik," he said. "In this country he is the equivalent of the SS commander and the Gestapo chief. Nina told me he's out here. He's on the tape. Committing murders personally."

Friel uttered an obscenity. "Ever seen so many teeth in one mouth?"

Night Runner's eyes narrowed. The corners of his mouth twitched in an almost-smile.

"Take him out?" Friel stroked the barrel of his smart gun.

"Yes," said Swayne. "But not the way you think."

Night Runner cocked his head. "Take him out of the country?"

Swayne nodded.

"I like it," said Night Runner.

"I'd rather whack him," said Friel. "What are we going to do? Take him back and put him on trial? So he can get a slap on the wrist and get some kind of diplomatic immunity or something? Let's whack him."

Swayne opened his mouth, but Night Runner spoke first. "Henry."

Friel glared at the Gunny.

"The captain says we're going to take him out of the country."

"Take him out of the country. That's what I say."

That settled, Swayne could not help feel a surge of confidence. Night Runner had done what Potts would have done. He might not like being in a leadership position, but he was a leader.

Swayne shared his plan for getting to Markocevik. He had cooked it up on the march to this point. His plan was short on detail and long on contingencies. The one thing they knew was that once they tried to get at Markocevik, such an important figure in the Serb hierarchy, the Serb Army would throw everything possible at them. So Swayne tried to have an answer for anything. As usual he gave his men latitude to react to unexpected situations on their own. For he knew that once the first shot was fired, the best military plan in the world and all its fallback positions were academic.

After he had gone over his outline twice, each time letting Night Runner and Friel chip in with their own observations, he made his decision. "We're going to do it." He looked into the eyes of both of his men, letting them know that he had finished listening and was now taking full responsibility—the Force Recon Team was no democracy, and no Marine officer was going to rule by popular vote.

After both men nodded to him, letting him know that they understood the terms under which they would fight, he said, "Now give me all the string and wire in your packs."

THE FOREST—1804 HOURS LOCAL

MARKOCEVIK TRAVELED AT the front of the column. The brigade commander's concern for his own safety, he thought, was misplaced. Because the general traveled close to the danger, the colonel had to as well. And *his* own safety was what he was more concerned about.

Nobody cared as much about that tape than he himself, Markocevik knew. In fact, if it were to fall into almost any hands in the world, it would cause trouble for him. If the Kosovars or NATO allies were to have it, of course there would be all that bad press and the calls for war-crimes trials. If his superiors—although there were very few in the country—were to get their hands on it, they might well find some way to remove him because the video proved that he was capable of such bad judgment, endangering the entire regime. Naturally, if his competitors, either in political circles or the military, were to get hold of it, they would use it to discredit him, perhaps selling it to the highest bidder. The one thing he had learned about being in a high position within his country—everybody else was eager to move him aside and take his spot.

Already he was feeling pressure from the president in his underground command center, where he had taken refuge to avoid NATO bombs.

The trouble was, many of those bombs had begun falling on precious military resources inside Kosovo. In part, due to Markocevik's own genius, the country had an elaborate system of tank decoys and other measures to neutralize the kind of bombing that had devastated Iraq in previous wars. The plan had been to shelter precious armored vehicles and aircraft, dispersing military units. Devices could create false heat signatures and make engine noises. Plywood tanks could be taken out of storage to create more than a dozen armored divisions overnight. If NATO wasted all their bombs on such decoys, that was to the advantage of the Serbs.

But if he continued to move his columns around during broad daylight, NATO would not waste time on decoys. One tank battalion had already been virtually destroyed. Several troop convoys traveling in trucks with no surface-to-air missile protection had been hit.

Markocevik checked the sky as a noisy Tomahawk missile thundered overhead at no more than two hundred feet. It would be dark in a few hours, and maybe they could continue to move on the roads freely. Or maybe by then he would have tracked down his enemy, the Americans.

Either way, he wasn't about to hide in some bunker or cave and give them the chance to get that woman and that tape out of the country.

His entire life had suddenly gone to the dogs. Literally. The handler's two bloodhounds had kept up baying for a full half hour now. The handler, a sergeant, kept assuring him that they were solidly on the trail of the woman.

Markocevik's aide-de-camp traveled with him, keeping a map handy. Now and then Markocevik would call a halt. The major would pinpoint their position. Markocevik would draw some lines on the map, marking their progress and possible routes the escapees might be following. He would then give orders over the radio for units to reposition.

The commanders—mostly colonels—always wanted to argue about exposing their units to nonstop air attacks.

Markocevik brushed aside every protest, becoming more impatient, making more serious threats.

By the end of the day, he had threatened to kill more people than NATO bombs had already taken out.

THE TRAIL TO MACEDONIA—1817 HOURS LOCAL

PERFECT HAD STUDIED the terrain and had done all he could to prepare himself in case it came down to a fight with the Serb squad below him. Behind him, he heard a noise, and turned to see Petr crawling on his belly toward him. He guessed that the man had been shot at enough times in his life to make him cautious.

Perfect backed away from his overlook and turned to talk to Petr in sign language, holding his arms as if he were shooting a rifle, then showing all his fingers to indicate the number of men, finally pointing over the slope.

Petr nodded as if he understood. He made the shape of a pistol with his right thumb and forefinger, then tapped his chest. Perfect shrugged and shook his head. He had no weapon to offer the man. Because of extra video equipment and gadgets, the team was not traveling with pistols on this mission.

He did remove a bayonet from his belt and offer it. Petr smiled and pushed at him with open hands. He wanted no part of hand-to-hand combat.

Suddenly Petr put his hands to his ears, and Perfect crawled back to his spot where he could see what was going on. He heard the sound of rattling gear as men got ready to move.

At first he was relieved to see that the Serbs felt safe enough to gather in a group. They passed around a couple of cigarettes and adjusted each other's gear. The squad leader talked on a handheld radio for a minute. He put the radio into a shirt pocket and turned to face Perfect as if he had known he was hiding there all the time.

The squad leader waved his arms, signaling his men to go up the hill. They protested. He growled at them.

Perfect's heart stopped. Exactly the worst situation he

could imagine. A voice in his head mocked him. On his first day in this country with the Force Recon Team, all he could do was think about personal glory. Then, after a shameful experience, he was only too glad to have a non-combat part of the mission, one that was important without any personal glory. Now this. A fight that he would not be able to avoid.

Perfect knew he had only seconds to act. The Serbs were going to come up that hill no matter what. There wasn't time to pick up the litter and run away. If he gave them the chance, they would spread out, and he would have no hope for holding his own with them. He brought his rifle to his shoulder, his thumb working the lever on the side of the breech so the gun would shoot on full automatic.

As he had been trained, he laid his sights on the groin of the squad leader, hoping that he was the only man with a radio. On the first burst, the barrel would rise. He would get control of it, but aiming low was to overcome the tendency to miss high.

As he prepared to pull the trigger, a single thought crossed his mind. Would he get out of Kosovo alive? Not that he would get medals or fame. Not that he cared all that much about the videotape. Or the victims of that atrocity. But would he survive?

The thought kept him from squeezing the slack out of the trigger.

He recognized the feeling taking hold of him. He tried to tell himself he was just thinking out the situation. But he knew the real word: panic.

THE FOREST—1829 HOURS LOCAL

SWAYNE'S STRATEGY FOR taking on a force that he knew to be so much larger seemed too complicated. He stationed Friel on an outcropping of rock well above the forest floor. From his spot he was to watch over the battle. Swayne didn't want him getting involved unless it was necessary to save one of the others. He saw the look of defiance on Friel's face when he laid out his plan. So he took an extra step of looking him in the eyes and repeating his orders: "Do not shoot until you are told to shoot, until one of us asks for your assistance."

Friel just stared at him.

"Henry?"

"Yes. Sir."

Swayne's job was to put himself directly into the path of the oncoming Serbs. Once they had made sure that Markocevik was using dogs to track them from the killing zone again, Swayne searched the ditch that they had navigated that morning. The spot he wanted gave him cover from behind a natural dam of boulders and tree stumps. Outside the ditch was a small ridge that would allow him to move laterally. Thus, he had two escape routes, one in the ditch and one behind the low ridge. Several fighting positions would let him shoot and move to keep the Serbs guessing as to the numbers of attackers and disposition of troops. He gave that a thought. Ridiculous. One man wasn't going to create enough resistance to hold the Serbs back long enough for the second part of his plan to take effect.

He tried to console himself that he was more than one man, being a Force Recon Marine. And they had picked up several assault rifles along the route, those left behind by the dead and wounded who had been hit by boomers this morning. He had positioned two of the rifles, one at each of his alternate firing positions. They would help create the impression of more men. Still. Reason and hope would have to fight it out among themselves. Because the nearing sounds of barking dogs indicated that combat was only minutes away.

•   •   •

FRIEL HAD PICKED his spot on the cliff above the action. He had done it quickly, so he would have more time for bitching. Here he was with his smart gun, the best damned weapon in the inventory, and Swayne wouldn't even let him pop a cap on the Serbs' asses.

Friel's smart gun, which he called his Blowpipe, held only six rounds in each clip. Each was a twenty-millimeter missile with a self-contained guidance system, each on a discrete frequency. Friel could designate a target either by a visible laser or IR beam. When he fired, a charge of compressed gas launched the tiny missile at subsonic speed, with no muzzle flash and little noise. Then a tiny rocket motor ignited and propelled the round to a high speed, and quickly. A homing device in the nose of the round would pick up the laser beam, then the target selected by Friel. It would recognize the target on its own by digital imaging. The missile locked on with the tenacity of a pit bull. It could follow the digital signature on the move at sixty miles an hour. Even if the target changed profile. If a walking man sank into a crouch, the round's memory would recognize it and compensate for the change in shape. In tests, Swayne had seen the device fired at target silhouettes that shifted from left profile, to a running man, to a diving man, to a prone, head-on image. The missile adjusted each time until it struck home. The only instance in which he had seen it go awry was when the man-target went behind a tree and disappeared from digital sight. So the missile had remained on point at the spot where the image had vanished. The armor-piercing sabot round punched a hole through the foot-thick hickory, slashed through the target, and buried itself twenty inches deep in solid limestone behind.

As the first round locked on, Friel could redesignate a second target. The gun would apply a new frequency to its laser, and a second missile could be fired before the first had struck its target. And a third—although this mission required only two kills. Piece of Granny's pound cake, as Gunny Potts used to say.

The thought of the Gunny pissed him off. The man was gone. He had saved Friel's life at the cost of his own.

One of these days they weren't going to have Friel to kick around anymore either. Maybe he was going to find a Force Recon unit that actually let him do some of the fighting. A team that would appreciate his ability to fight, to shoot. To kill. No more of these Sneaky Pete missions. Why was it that everybody else in the Marine Corps could bend a rule anytime he wanted to, but just one little blink and they'd get all over *his* ass like stink on shit?

Shit.

THE TRAIL TO MACEDONIA—1833 HOURS LOCAL

PERFECT WASN'T EVEN thinking about aimed fire. All he wanted to do was get off as many rounds as he could as quickly as he could, filling the Serbs with slugs. As many as possible in one blast. That was what he was supposed to do. That was what he wanted to do.

He reminded himself to keep the trigger down until all thirty rounds had been spat out. Then reload. He checked beside him to see that his last boomer had been armed and was ready to throw—Swayne had taken all his others and had thrown them into the forest earlier today. The one would have to do. All he had to do was pick it up, touch the button to start the countdown, and toss it. He was ready. He was more than ready.

When he looked back at the Serbs, the squad had just begun dispersing. No more time to spare. No time to think. This was it.

Still, he continued putting off the fateful moment, as if the problem would go away if he waited.

They had trained him in all the right ways. He knew exactly what to do in this situation.

What they had not been able to do was to put him into a realistic situation, one that would mimic actual combat.

Trained he was. Ready he was not.

Perfect began to tremble. Before his eyes the tactical situation began to disintegrate. In only a few seconds more, he would not be able to get more than a couple men on the first burst. The rest would hit the ground, seek cover, reorganize, and come up the hill after him.

He knew it. He saw it unfolding. Yet he could not make himself pull the trigger. Shame washed over him. He was going to fail. He was going to—

He felt a hand on a shoulder, and turned around to look into the eyes of Petr. The man spoke to him in his language. Perfect told him he did not understand, and he did not like the sound of whining in his own voice. The man took Perfect's face in his left hand and squeezed, hard. He turned Perfect's face toward the enemy, shook it, and slapped him on the back, giving him another command.

He was telling him to shoot.

Perfect knew what had to be done. Still, he could not make himself do it.

Petr hit him on the head and shouted. What he said could not be anything but an obscenity.

"Shut up, you idiot, they'll hear you," Perfect growled.

Perfect looked to his right and saw Petr standing upright, giving the one-finger gesture of obscenity to the Serbs, the international insult that transcended all languages. All the while he shouted at them, and Perfect did not need to know what was being said. He could tell they were obscenities.

Perfect could not believe what was happening. This man was showing more courage than he could muster.

For a second the forest was silent. The Kosovar stopped shouting. The men, Perfect could see, ten of them, looked up at Petr in astonishment, their eyes wide open. Even the birds and squirrels had gone quiet in the forest.

To Perfect it felt as if he were looking at a picture, something abstract, no, surreal. This was not happening, and he was not in it.

To his left, he heard a noise of footsteps in the leaves. He saw Gus moving into the open. The dog barked at the Serbs.

Even the dog had more courage? That notion was all that Perfect needed.

All at once the forest erupted, as he clenched his finger on the trigger and sprayed bullets down the line of Serbs. Once he had passed the squad leader, Perfect realized that he needed to go back and finish off the man with the radio, who was lying on his side, clawing at his jacket. Perfect realized he was trying to get the radio out of his pocket.

Before he could lay the sights of his chattering rifle on the man, his gun stopped firing. He gripped it harder. Harder. But it would not fire again. He felt a slap on the head and thought he had been shot. No, Petr had slapped him. The Kosovar grasped his gun and pushed the magazine-ejection lever. Of course! He was out of ammunition.

He picked up the magazine, which was taped to a second banana clip, reversed it, and re-inserted it into the rifle. He fired another thirty rounds on full automatic and took out a third clip. This he jammed into his rifle, and emptied half of it into the sergeant as he fumbled with his radio.

By now Serbs had begun returning fire.

Petr stuck a fist in Perfect's face. No, it was a grenade, the boomer. Perfect had forgotten it. He took it away, glanced at the digital timer—and felt his heart stop.

Petr had accidentally set its timer off already.

There were only two seconds to go. Perfect tossed it downhill and to his left. He hoped that he had thrown it far enough and in the right direction so that it would cause some damage to the Serbs.

Suddenly he wondered about Gus. But that thought entered his head just about the time a wave of concussion slapped his face. No matter how much it hurt, it set him into action once more. He rolled away from the edge of his overlook, pulled another magazine, reloaded, and ran to his right, toward the right end of the Serb squad, opposite where the grenade had gone off.

He heard firing from below. From what he could tell were no more than three rifles. If only he hadn't been frozen, he could have finished off even those three. This time, though, he slapped his own head to get such an idea out of his head. There was nothing left to do to get back the opportunities that he had lost. He need not worry about redeeming himself in the eyes of the Force Recon Team or the Marine Corps anymore. He had to restore his own self-respect.

He reached a tree that had sprung up with split trunks. He wedged his body into the space. Carefully he looked over the slope, and saw two men moving laterally to get away from the killing zone. One of them stopped behind a tree, part of his body exposed. He was digging in a canvas case on his belt. He pulled out a radio. But before he could raise it to his mouth, his lips had exploded in blood. A second man, looking frightened and confused, turned around on the slope. Perfect wasted no time wasting him, stitching him up the side. Perfect hid behind the tree, trying to remember where he might have heard the third shooter's gun. Then he remembered he should not be thinking about this at all. Now that he had revealed his position, it was time to move. He dove to the ground. As he crawled on his belly, working his way downslope, he heard something crash on the trail up above him. Seconds later, a grenade went off behind the tree where he had shown a second of hesitation.

A wave of giddiness ran through him. *He had done something right.* Maybe it wasn't perfect, but he had actually done something smart. As he slithered under a low wall of bushes thick as any hedge, he saw motion to his left. Not one, but two men were maneuvering uphill toward the tree—he had miscounted. There were more men then he had thought. They kept firing at the split trunks, kept all their focus there.

Perfect felt sorry for them for a second. They were making mistakes of the kind he had made today and yesterday. But he did not feel sorry for long. He raised his rifle and waited. As one man tried to overlap the second, they were for a moment practically in line. Perfect squeezed one burst at the first man, who jerked away and fell over backward, falling down the slope, giving Perfect a clean shot at the second.

This man's rifle swung quickly. But it was not fast enough. Perfect's aim was off, so he did not hit center of mass. Instead he hit the arm and snapped it off at the wrist, leaving it to dangle by shreds of muscle and sinew.

Still, the Serb kept turning, his rifle held in one arm now. Perfect ignored the bizarre sight and concentrated on the center of the man's chest. He squeezed off a burst of six that started at the man's collarbone, ran up his neck, tore through his head, and took off his helmet.

Perfect was awed by the sight of destruction that he had caused. But he would not allow himself to concentrate on it. He swung his gun around looking for other sources of danger. Then he remembered he was making the same mistake again, and dove to his right, coming up in a firing position on both knees. He moved from position to position until within five minutes he had cleared the entire area, finding all twelve bodies, all twelve men dead.

A combination of emotions hit him. He felt like

throwing up. And he felt like laughing. But what he did was begin to weep. He had almost shamed himself. But one brave unarmed man had pulled him back from the brink. And a dog, his dog, had barked, allowing him to save his own soul.

THE FOREST—1847 HOURS LOCAL

SWAYNE KEPT WISHING his enemies would not come. At least not yet. There was too much daylight left in this sorry afternoon.

But as the sounds of barking dogs grew louder, he understood that he could not wish himself out of the situation. This was one of those inevitable jams where the only way to get to the exit sign was to fight.

He had positioned himself in the line of first fire. The Serbs would be following the dogs, of course. He'd guessed that they would travel spread out to cover a wide front. But he had chosen a spot where the terrain funneled all the easy routes into a bottleneck about fifty feet wide.

Besides, he knew the tendency of men. If they were traveling on a line, they would naturally concentrate anytime the barking of the dogs grew faint. So, if the animals were running through thick forest, their sounds would be dampened. Eventually the entire group would be traveling in a clump, if the officers and noncoms were not on the ball.

The first man came into view only twenty yards away. From what Swayne could hear, the nearest men behind him might be another twenty yards back. Swayne gritted his teeth that the Serb scout was doing his job, keeping ahead of the main force. By the time the scout got to Swayne, he would be in position to alert the others before they could be hit.

Swayne re-figured his situation. He had been hoping

to catch a group of men in the open and drop them with a single burst. With luck, the dogs would also be close enough so he could take them out. That was important. Even if Markocevik's force was to take out the trio of Spartans, without his dogs he would be set back, possibly for hours. Plenty of time for Perfect to get to his rally point.

Once the firing began, the normal reaction would be for the Serbs to find cover, diving into low areas and behind trees and fallen logs. Swayne had positioned the last half-dozen boomers into those most likely spots. On the ground at his elbow lay his computer with six pre-programmed signals ready to be transmitted. Each one would set off one of the concussion grenades nearby, catching some of the Serbs. If Swayne's plan had worked the way he wanted it, he would have wiped out nearly every man who could see where the action was coming from. It would take a few minutes for other men in the force to reorganize and determine how they had been hit. By then Swayne would have moved into his secondary fighting position.

One alert Serb soldier doing his job properly prevented his plan from taking effect. Swayne had to give him his grudging respect. If he were ever to get out of this situation alive, he would make it a teaching point for every Force Recon Marine. Hell, he would integrate that insight into every training program in the entire Marine Corps. One man doing his job properly could upset an enemy every time. Every Marine doing his or her job properly could beat an unbeatable force.

On the other hand, Swayne wasn't going to let this one man defeat his plan. He reordered priorities. The entire history of successful fighters was written in the ability to adjust a plan according to an enemy's action.

So he ignored the solitary scout, now just fifteen feet away. Maybe he would pass by. If so, Swayne would deal with him one way. If not, he would deal with him another way.

He saw that the man was moving quickly—too quickly to be effective as a scout. He could not jog through the forest and still see all that he had to see. Somebody was putting pressure on him to stay ahead of the dogs.

Swayne lowered his head when the scout was a mere five strides away. The man wasn't going to bypass him. In fact, he was about to step on him.

Fine, thought Swayne. Deal with him a third way.

THE TRAIL TO MACEDONIA—1853 HOURS

AFTER HE HAD collected himself, Perfect found the Kosovar named Petr getting the woman ready to travel again. No matter what Perfect had learned from this first combat experience, no matter how high he had flown nor how low he had fallen in his emotions, Petr was unimpressed.

Perfect realized, of course, that this was a man who had lived in the dread of combat day in, day out. And he also understood that they had to clear the area as quickly as possible. He might have prevented the Serbs from making a radio report. But the sounds of the firefight still reverberated in his ears, if not the forest. Somebody would be trying to make a net call, ordering every unit on the radio network to report whether it was the source of the gunfire. And enough units were scattered around the forest for some other patrol to start moving this way, making reports of their own.

Whether this patrol answered or not, the woods would soon be swarming with Serbs headed toward the spot.

In minutes they were on their way with the litter. In the adrenaline rush, Perfect felt that the wounded woman had lost half her weight. He felt strong enough to carry the litter by himself. If necessary, he could grab the woman, throw her over his shoulder, and fly her to safety. That was how good he felt.

Until a man stepped out of the forest not ten feet away and pointed a rifle at him. He froze, both hands on the handles of the litter. His rifle was slung across his back. Even as he thought of a way to get to it, two more men stepped onto the trail, again with rifles level. Then three more. They kept appearing until he stopped counting at twenty.

It didn't matter. One would have been enough. He was in no position to fight back.

In the sudden adrenaline crash that came next, he thought he might drop the wounded woman. His knees buckled, and he knelt, lowering her to the ground. When he looked up, an AK-47 rifle bore stared at him from the side, not more than six inches away.

The code of Force Recon did not permit a man to surrender. He might have been stupid before, but he would never be branded a surrendering coward. His hands flinched as he thought again of how he might get to his rifle. But that possibility vanished as the man with the AK-47 began tightening his forefinger on the pistol grip of the AK-47.

Three things happened at once.

Perfect groaned.

Petr shouted one of his curses.

The assault rifle went off in Perfect's face.

THE FOREST—1859 HOURS LOCAL

WITHOUT TAKING HIS eyes off the scout, Swayne felt for the first of the function keys on his computer, and mashed it emphatically as the scout was only three steps away.

When the first boomer went off, the scout dove at him,

partly in surprise, partly by instinct to get down, and partly by the sheer concussion of a grenade going off behind him.

Swayne rolled aside, letting the man hit the spot where he had been lying.

While he was in the air, the scout saw where he was about to land, saw the motion of an enemy rolling over, saw that he would have to act quickly to save his own life, either by firing or shouting. He also saw the point of a bayonet coming up to meet his face. At the last second the knife drove into his throat at the point where the two collarbones met. He hit the ground, landing first on the hilt of the bayonet, driving it into his spine just above the shoulder blades, severing the spinal cord. He lay on the ground beside Swayne, not dying immediately, but watching the Marine lieutenant act to kill his brother soldiers without his being able to lift a finger—literally—to stop it.

When Swayne saw the tip of his bayonet come out of the man's back, he wrote him off as a factor.

As he knew men would, the Serbs began firing without having a target. The safest thing to do, fearful men thought, was to shoot from a position of cover to hold back an enemy, at least to make him keep his head down.

That might be true. Or it might not. Swayne wasn't concerned about what they were thinking, only that they were firing. Mostly into the air, mostly without looking. He had memorized every fighting position during his recon of the area. He decided to wait until men lying on flat ground feeling exposed could get up and run toward better cover.

He heard shouting. Some were cries of the injured. Others were obviously orders. Then came the sound of rushing feet, boots clattering through the forest, men congregating behind logs and trees, in ditches, in the streambed, and in holes.

One angry voice kept shouting at the Serbs, obviously trying to organize them.

But that man could not regain command over all the firing going on. After seeing the scout doing so well at his job, Swayne was glad for the lack of discipline among the other Serbs.

More men began shouting. More orders. Definitely trying to organize. The gunfire slackened. Soon it stopped.

Swayne, his finger poised above his miniature keyboard, waited. If he could buy a few minutes, so much the better. If he could keep the Serbs pinned to this spot for even twenty minutes, the team would be twenty minutes closer to nightfall. By day he had little hope that they could succeed at what he was trying to pull off.

"Spartan One, report."

Zavello! *What a time for him to intervene.*

"Spartan One, this is Eagle One, transmitting in the blind. We have identified a radio signal. If it is yours, let me know at the first possible occasion, so I can keep NATO bombers off your backs."

Swayne had to smile. They had picked up the brief signal that he had sent to detonate the boomer. The one-eyed colonel had to have been sitting at the command operations desk two hundred feet below Quantico for a day and a half. What energy that man had.

Swayne turned on his radio. It didn't matter now that the Serbs could pinpoint his radio communications. All hell would break loose in a few minutes anyhow. Keeping his eyes and ears tuned to the most dangerous half-dozen positions from which the Serbs could attack, he began a report to Zavello. He started by giving the rally point and situation. He told his boss that the three of them would be engaging the Serbs at their present location to give Perfect time to get clear. Even as he spoke, he decided to keep his mouth shut about the plan to kidnap Markocevik. The idea was too outrageous to say. He did mention Nina. But only as a witness to the mass killings. He tried to get his mind off her, but could not, even as he noticed a Serb soldier stand up ten yards away and begin pointing and shouting, trying to get his troops to spread out and flank Swayne on both sides.

That was all it took to get Nina out of his mind.

THE TRAIL TO MACEDONIA—1915 HOURS LOCAL

NINA HAD FELT the shower in her state of dreamy semiconsciousness. At first she was glad for the cool mist. But when she opened her eyes, she realized she was looking at the head of a dead man. The spray had been his blood. She saw the uniform and recognized it from previous trips to the field.

The dead man was a Force Recon Marine.

Jack?

No, the strands of hair that were visible, those strands that had not been discolored by blood, were black. Swayne was blond. This was not Jack. She felt a mixture of relief and shame. Glad that it was not her lover. Ashamed that she could be glad another man had died.

She heard shouting. Did not understand it. The language seemed to be the mush that Markocevik spoke.

She felt herself fading. Her lips tingled. She kept waiting for the light. Wasn't there a bright light at the end of the tunnel? Wasn't that the last thing you saw as you crossed over?

Deep inside her head she snickered. Crossing over? When had she ever believed there was anyplace over? It did not pay for somebody like her to believe in heaven. For that would require believing in the other place. Which was the more likely destination for somebody in her career field to end up.

A cold, wet cloth was being used to wash her face.

She tried to open her mouth to ask for water. She thought of some kind of smart remark: *Why waste water cleaning me up when I could be drinking it?*

But she could not speak the words, could not even open her mouth. For her dry lips were glued together.

Until a dampened fingertip with water on it forced an opening.

More drops of water from the finger seeped between her lips, loosening her tongue from the roof of her mouth.

She tried to say thanks, but all she heard was a hiss escape her throat.

Then somebody spoke to her in broken English. At first the words did not register. It was rough English, thick with an accent, and difficult to understand. But on her last outing, she had grown adept at understanding the Iraqi gibberish that passed for English.

So the second time she made sense of the accent and understood the words: "So sorry, madam. Truly."

The sound of an apology opened her eyes as much as anything. She did not recognize the man, but she recognized the look. He was truly sorry. But for what? She tried to ask, but could not form the words.

"Shoot man, big accident. Shoot American soldier. So sorry, madam, kill soldier. Truly."

Then she felt tears forming in her eyes. These men were not going to kill her, as Markocevik had tried. But they had killed a Marine. Perhaps they thought he was a Serb. She could not know. She was glad that she might survive this after all. But after all that she had seen—and now this—she did not know whether she wanted to awaken someday to try to make sense of it.

The man stepped away from her. She could not move her head, but somebody lifted it for her and put a cup of cool water to her mouth. She let the water flow down. And with her head in the air, she saw men going through the pockets of the dead Marine. At the sight of them taking his belongings, she began to weep. But she still did not have strength to protest.

But when one of the men held up a videotape cassette—*the* videotape cassette, a sound did escape her lips.

Two men argued over the tape, and she used the last of her strength to call to them.

As they leaned down to her, she felt the light closing into a pinpoint before her eyes. She was going to pass out and knew it.

So she spoke quickly, as forcefully as she could. "That tape is mine. Give it to me."

As the tunnel of light closed like the diaphragm of a camera lens to black, she heard her answer in rough English: "No, madam, this tape is ours. Truly."

She screamed at them.

But it was from deep inside a tunnel. So far gone was she that the sound could not rise even to her own ears. And then she was gone to blackness, as if the black-and-white television of her life had blinked off.

THE FOREST—1928 HOURS LOCAL

FRIEL HAD TO loosen his grip on his smart gun to scratch his right forefinger. It had grown itchy, literally. Waiting. Nothing ate at the keen edge of a sniper worse than this. Nothing was worse than waiting. A shooter did not want to be the last man at the table when there was a fight going on. It pissed him off that the captain had decided to take on the Serbs all by himself. Officers. Always taking advantage of the good stuff, leaving scraps to the enlisted. If Swayne kept it up, there wouldn't be enough Serbs for Friel to kill. He'd been in this damned country for two days getting fired at by artillery, bombed by his own planes, and insulted by

getting all the shit jobs. And never once getting to fire
a shot in anger.

SWAYNE COULD SEE the man waving his arms was an
officer. The man found little success in yelling. And
since Swayne hadn't reacted to his standing up, the officer felt brave, perhaps thinking that they had been hit
by a booby trap. So he came clear of cover altogether,
trying to show his men that it was safe to get out of
their positions and move. It was a brave and foolish
thing to do, and Swayne could not help but admire his
courage. And it worked, because the bushes on both
sides of him had begun to rustle.

Swayne tried to read the collective mind of his enemy.
Sure, if the officer was not getting shot, it must be safe.
*Yes, if the officer says it was a booby trap, that seems
likely. Wasn't that what happened to the men this morning?*

The officer's radio crackled, and Swayne could hear
an angry voice shouting at him. He hoped it was Markocevik. And he saw that it could have been, for the
officer became animated. He shouted and waved franti-
cally to get his troops on the move again. Swayne could
understand but a single word of the message spewed by
the officer. But that one word spoke volumes: *Markocevik.*

Swayne swept his fingers across the function keys of
his handheld computer like a pianist rippling down the
keys. A chain of explosions went off. Swayne was nest-
ling into the ground by then, so he did not see what
happened. But he could guess. Men standing or kneeling. Explosions going off in the bottom of holes, or at
face level in the bushes near the best positions of cover.

He had clasped his hands over his ears to protect them
from the concussion. But when he stood up, all was
silent. Except for the falling of leaves and twigs. And

that angry voice still transmitting over the radio to deaf ears.

The gunfire started up again, but this time there were no rifles or pistols firing within thirty yards of his position. Swayne realized there were no men alive or conscious within the radius for anyone to be able to point and shoot a rifle. This firing came from other forces farther back, people who did not know what was going on, men who were frightened by what they had heard or not heard. Terrified and worried. Terrified because the silence could only mean somebody had died on the trail ahead. Worried that they might be next.

These things ran through Swayne's mind quickly, even as he ran quickly, clearing the position. He knew the standard procedure for a situation like this. The Serb unit would very likely pull back to a safe distance and pound the forest with artillery.

So Swayne did not run away from the enemy force. Rather, he ran toward it, trying to ignore the devastation he had caused, trying not to see how the scattered bodies lay, trying not to hear cries of pain. He was glad that he could not understand the Serb language. He did not want to have to listen to men calling in agony for their mothers.

Once he got beyond the spot where men had died, he moved into his secondary position, a rabbit tunnel through a tangle of thorny vines. He could get into his spot only by crawling on his belly. And to prevent his pack from catching, he had thrown away everything that he could spare. Then he pushed the tight bundle ahead of him. Once it was at arm's reach, he shoved his rifle ahead. He worked his way into the tight spot six inches at a time. The foliage was so dense that not even the light filtered into it. The tunnel was curved and had several branches, so that a man could not get down on his knees and spot him either. And no soldier in a hurry, forced by his commanders to keep going into the teeth of gunfire, was going to risk trying to weave his way through.

Swayne had figured all the angles. Even if his enemy were to be ordered into the tangle, their feet would not touch the ground as they walked over it. They would have to climb over it like a haystack. A haystack with spines. If a man got caught in it and thrashed around, he would bleed to death before he could get out. The only way they were going to get him was to try to drive a tank over it or set his hiding place on fire. But by then, the next part of his plan would have gone into effect, and the Serbs would be running by this spot at full speed.

FRIEL FELT LIKE Wile E. Coyote with the Rube Goldberg setup that Swayne had told him to arrange. He was a killer, not a cartoon character. What the captain wanted him to do was pull a stunt so ridiculous that it would be too embarrassing even to talk about later on in the debriefing. Here he was, maybe the best shooter in the Marine Corps, maybe even in the whole world. He had a gun that could knock out tanks, if the shot was placed perfectly—which, with him, it always was. Two or three missions ago, he had even sunk a submarine with it. *A sub-freakin'-marine!* Another story so incredible that he could not tell it because nobody would believe it.

But here he lay, with a bundle of strings in his hand, not even looking for targets through the scope of the deadly smart gun. What a dick way to fight. The captain was always saying the enemy wasn't going to do what you expected him to. But here he was, trying to pull off some goofy plan that depended on just that—

The artillery started up on schedule. Just as the captain said it would. Okay, so Swayne wasn't an ordinary officer. So maybe he had proved that he could be right on one thing today. Okay, he had been right on other things, too, on previous missions. But the rest of the plan? How was something as goofy as that going to come off?

He slithered sideways into a deep space in the layers of rock on the side of the cliff. Until he felt like a wedge, and the ripple of explosions hitting the ground a couple hundred yards away reverberated through him.

He put his head on his forearm and tried to keep the thought out of his mind that the side of the mountain was going to vibrate off. It would crush him first, then bury him under eighty kabillion pounds of rocks. Nobody was ever going to find anything of him but a freaking grease spot with Boston crab cakes in his trousers.

Anybody who's ever been in an artillery attack can only think of one thing—that it will be soon be over, Friel thought. At least that was what other people had told him. And what he had felt every time he'd been in the shit like today. But this time there was something new. Anytime now, his own guys up above might start dropping bombs. Artillery was one thing to shake down the side of a mountain. If those bombs ever started falling, he was going to die here like a squished ant.

Kosovo. What a godforsaken place. If he ever got out of the joint alive, he was never coming back, not even if they turned the whole country into a parking lot for the biggest Cabela's store in the world.

THE TRAIL TO MACEDONIA—1949 HOURS LOCAL

NINA WAS AWARE of the distant pounding of artillery. She had been on the receiving end of it in the past, and understood its rumble. Of more concern to her was the pain she was now feeling. Obviously, she was getting better. Otherwise, how could she feel so miserable? She had taken on more water, and even a few bites of some salty canned meat. But only a few bites that she could barely swallow.

Except for one thing, she would rather die than suffer this pain.

For the first time in her life that one thing was not personal achievement, being recognized as the top journalist in the world. She didn't even care all that much about the tape.

She just wanted to see Jack Swayne one more time. She did not even need to survive to be satisfied. Just a minute or two with Jack before she died. That would be enough.

THE FOREST—1956 HOURS LOCAL

THE ARTILLERY SHIFTED, and Friel saw that the captain had been right two times in a row. Pretty awesome. The odds against any officer being right that often under any conditions were too high for him to calculate. But in a combat situation—

Friel murmured a curse word. The Serbs were not even trying to run down the center of the bottleneck anymore. Instead of following their artillery as it rolled back, the soldiers were claiming the sides of the hills— he checked both slopes—both sides of the valley, trying to run a giant pincer movement. Just like the captain said they would. Friel would have liked to turn on his radio mike to tell the boss he had been right. But that would draw artillery fire, so he had to keep his mouth shut.

He eased out of his hiding place and laid his smart gun aside. He picked up the four strings that he had laid on the ground and held with a stone.

Each string was tied to the trigger of an AK-47 assault rifle that the team had picked up on the forest floor. Each rifle was strapped to a tree in the forest with bad-ass duct tape. Each rifle had been aimed at a spot where Serb soldiers would travel, should they try to flank the team.

Friel had a position almost a hundred yards away from

the guns, a maneuver that took every inch of string and wire in the packs of the three Spartans.

That captain. He had picked the spot, and the Serbs were following his script as if Swayne had been in their command post giving them orders over the radio. Maybe officers were not such slackers after all. He gave that a second thought. Shit, yes, they were. Swayne was just an exception to the rule.

The Serbs didn't cooperate perfectly, of course. Their timing was off, and he would have to give Swayne a bad time about that when this operation was over. Two platoons were passing through one area at the same time, and only a squad was filing through a second firing zone. A third group was too far behind to get to their spot on time. And it didn't look as if the fourth zone would ever be occupied.

Still. Friel tensed. He wished he could shift some of his firepower. He even thought about picking up his smart gun and adding to the damage.

But the captain would have his ass for that. The whole idea of this shady maneuver was to give the enemy a bogus position for them to maneuver against. If he somehow got spotted, artillery would be on him too fast for him to escape.

Friel decided. This was as good a concentration as he could expect. He wished that he had remembered which string went to which rifle. But he did not. So he yanked them all at once, laying down a burst of fire on all four areas.

The only effect he could see was in one zone where the Serbs had sent far too many men into the open. His first burst of fire sent the whole crew scattering, but almost a dozen men sprawled in the open, many of them apparently hit.

Friel waited for the Serbs to return fire on the fake ambush. He wished he could have had one of Force Recon's patented Acme ambush kits, which were capa-

ble of laying down an entire firefight. But since they had
not expected any enemy contact on this mission, they
had not brought one.

Friel had calculated he would have three or four bursts
for his attack. Although the bad guys had cleared out of
the two areas where they were vulnerable, they didn't
seem to realize that a third area was also a danger zone,
and some of them tried to run across it.

So he gave them a second burst, this time knocking
down two more men.

He had to grin. Those poor bastards. They didn't have
a clue that they were being shot by some guy from Boston pulling strings like the puppet master in some cheap-
ass movie.

Before he could get off the third burst, artillery began
to rain on the phony ambush. Friel nodded in appreciation. That was a pretty fast reaction. He jerked his
strings to empty the magazines of his remote-control rifles. He didn't get much out of them. Two of the strings
had been cut by artillery fire. The third gun did not fire
at all. And the fourth only shot off about six rounds.

But to his astonishment, one more Serb—a nitwit that
had climbed a tree—took a header from thirty feet up
and landed on his neck. Friel had no way of knowing
whether the guy just fell or jumped or whether he had
been hit. But from the way he lay motionless, it was all
the same. Friel laughed through an obscenity. What was
the letter home going to say? *Dear Mom, your asshole
son was so freaking stupid he took a swan dive right
straight to moron hell?*

Friel wiped the grin off his face. Literally. The captain
would have his ass for making jokes about shit such as
that. *Get down to business,* he told himself. *Before you
get too cocky and somebody writes a letter home about
your moron ass.*

His job now was to stay out of the fight until he heard
from Swayne. He jerked the strings hard to break them

off, and began to reel them in so they wouldn't leave a
trail to his hiding place. This was the most ridiculous
plan that the captain had ever come up with. Sure,
Swayne had been right about how the Serbs would react
to the artillery and the fake ambush. But what did that
prove? The next words out of his mouth, if the captain
was right—and that was a big if—would split the team
up one more time. Ridiculous. Sending Friel to catch up
with Perfect so he could baby-sit him. The best shot on
the team. The Marine with the most kills. The one guy
they could always depend on in a fight. And this time
they weren't even going to let him into it. Just like an
officer. Just like a gunnery sergeant. Instead he had to
run back, catch up to the sick, lame, and lazy—the
woman, the Kosovar, and Perfect. Not to mention that
dog he rode in on.

What a shit job. Kosovo was nothing more than one
shit job after another. How much longer was he supposed to put up with this crap?

MARKOCEVIK HAD LEFT his SUV and walked only a
hundred meters before running into the first battle zone.
To the sides of the trail lay men who had been flattened
by some sort of booby trap. From the look of their bleeding ears, concussion grenades. Except for a man's arm
dripping strings of blood from a tree limb, a pistol still
gripped in that dead hand, a sight that made him smile
with the irony of a sight gag, he showed no emotion.
He had seen enough dead people, had contributed to
enough deaths, and had seen enough grotesque images
to inoculate him forever against the sight of suffering.

Not even the image of a soldier lying gutted, his heart
still beating in the open air, could distract his attention.

He was intent on moving forward. Already the dog
handler was making excuses that the artillery smoke was
dulling the animals' noses and that the explosions had
created areas where the woman's scent had been oblit-

erated. Markocevik's only concession to that complaint was to have the artillery shifted to the spot where the ambush had taken place. He summoned his brigade commander and demanded that the troops pick up the pace.

The colonel argued that he was instructing his subordinate officers to maneuver against the attackers. Markocevik was having none of it. He wanted to push on through. They stood in sight of that beating heart, and the image kept distracting the colonel's attention. Markocevik told him to forget about the ambush and push forward. He wanted to reestablish the trail the woman had followed.

"I will lose more men like that one," the colonel said, pointing to the gutted man. He ordered Markocevik's aide-de-camp to order that medics be sent up to care for the soldier.

"I suggest you forget him," Markocevik said, his tone making clear that it was not a suggestion at all. "Push your officers to move forward, Colonel, or else they will be buried in this forest. There will be no hospital for the wounded. There will be no evacuation for the dying. There will be no letters home. Only a bulldozer plowing a ditch in the forest. Only a pile of bodies burned with gasoline. If I do not catch that woman, nobody in your unit will see the morning." The colonel, his eyes wide at the brazen threat and the disregard for the lives of his men, was faced with a life's choice. His life. His choice.

He told his adjutant to order units forward as quickly as possible, whether there was gunfire or not.

Markocevik smirked. Of course the colonel gave in to him. Men—and women—always gave in to him.

The colonel stared at Markocevik, but not for long. He had been disgraced. His men had been spent needlessly, as far as he was concerned. He had not said enough to prevent the waste of his soldiers. But he had said enough to ensure the waste of his own career.

Markocevik, always keen to read weakness in other

men, saw the combination of disgrace and defiance in the colonel's eyes. He might be in a hurry, but there was always time to kneel in the dust beside an opponent that he had vanquished on the arena floor, place a knife to the throat, and finish him.

"Colonel Stojkovic, you are no longer in command of this brigade. Neither are you a colonel. You are my driver. Go tell my former driver to come forward—he was once a colonel of infantry. He will take command of your unit. You will take command of my vehicle. As you will see, it needs a thorough cleaning and waxing once we get back to garrison."

His command did not have the effect that Markocevik expected. Instead of dismay, the colonel's eyes widened only slightly, and a smile creased his face.

Markocevik started to ask why the former colonel had not moved, but he saw that the man's eyes were looking over his shoulder.

He turned and saw what the colonel had seen, but his eyes would not comprehend it.

"Not possible," he said.

But it did, indeed, seem possible. For the gutted man, a man in the uniform of a Serb soldier, had stood up, and his intestines had fallen to the ground. Yet the man seemed whole. He walked toward Markocevik, whose mouth tried to form around words that would not be spoken. Markocevik's eyes tried to read sense into the vision. But he could not.

Until Night Runner raised his right hand with the Bedouin sword, faked a downward stroke, and met Markocevik's ducking chin with a left uppercut. Markocevik's knees buckled. He started to fall forward, but Night Runner struck him in the forehead with an elbow and laid him out on his back.

The colonel's hand went to the pistol in its holster on his right hip. Night Runner raised the sword. The colonel folded his arms.

"Are you one of the Americans we have been chasing?" he asked, his English tinged with a British accent.

"Yes," said Swayne, stepping out of the underbrush. "We're both Americans. We don't have to kill you, but we will. We want him."

The colonel smiled. "He's a butcher. He kills Kosovars. Women. Old men. Children. My soldiers. Finish him, if you like. Or if you'd rather, I will kill him myself."

Swayne shook his head. "We're not going to kill him. We're going to take him back for trial as a war criminal."

The colonel seemed disappointed. "For all the bloody good that will do." He shrugged. "He has friends in the West. I doubt he will ever go on trial."

Swayne bit his lip. The man was probably right, but this was no time to debate it. "Give me your pistol."

The colonel did as he was told, and Swayne cleared the weapon and handed it back.

"Shouldn't you kill me so I don't sound the alarm?" said the man, putting his pistol away.

"Yes, I should. But that would be murder." Swayne pulled a patch of bad-ass duct tape from his jacket. Night Runner came up with a handful of nylon pull-ties. "It will be enough to disable you, Colonel. We're taking Markocevik. You're going to give us a head start."

Swayne wished that Friel was in the forest, that he had disobeyed orders so he could watch over them at a time like this. But he had ordered Friel to join up with the others. Henry, no matter how much he hated being left out of a fight, would already be long gone.

"Somebody is coming," Night Runner whispered.

"Give us until dark," said Swayne, approaching the officer with his strip of tape.

"Take him into the woods if you must," said the colonel. "But I have a better idea. Here, use those bowels as you used them before. Only on him."

• • •

WHEN MARKOCEVIK'S AIDE-DE-CAMP returned to report to the general that orders had been carried out, he was stunned to find his boss lying on his back, his shirt ripped open, and his intestines pouring out onto the ground, covered with dirt. Two soldiers kept trying to shove Markocevik's guts back into him, and they were not being too careful about it.

He hollered at them in his language, and the colonel barked at him in return. When the major did not respond, the colonel pulled his pistol. That the major understood. He ran back toward the rear.

"I told him that if Markocevik dies, he will spend the rest of his life cleaning toilets. I sent him back for a vehicle to take us out of here. The aide-de-camp will have to ride with us. Keep your faces in the dark."

"What if he makes us?" Swayne said.

"Makes us?"

"Sorry. What if he recognizes that we are not Serbs?"

The colonel shrugged. "Do with him as you will. But he is a weak man. He will speak out against Markocevik with very little pressure. If you take him alive as well, you will have a witness against Markocevik's most intimate, most deadly orders and behaviors."

Night Runner and Swayne traded glances and shook their heads at once.

"Too many people to handle," Swayne said. "We won't be able to take him with us."

The colonel nodded. "Yes, you will. Wait and see."

"How can I trust you?" Swayne wanted to know.

The colonel said his name. "Sava Stojkovic. Do you recognize it from your intelligence reports?"

Swayne did. Stojkovic was a soldier, Swayne said to Night Runner.

The colonel said, "I have always been a soldier. And a soldier does not kill innocent people. You can understand that. It is the basis for your trust. Is it not?"

Swayne bit his lip. Trust a Serb? Why would he? But trust a soldier? Why not?

"I see in your face already that you will trust me without your having to say the words. That is good."

"Will you come with us?" Swayne wanted to know.

"I have to. Either they will kill me because I let Markocevik be captured while he was in the security of my brigade. Or he will send a message back through his friends in the West, and I will be killed."

"And if you betray us—" Swayne started to say.

"Feel free to kill me yourself." He put a finger to his lips. "They're coming."

The aide-de-camp returned with a driver carrying a litter. The colonel directed them to hand over the litter to Swayne and Night Runner, who dragged Markocevik's limp body onto it. The colonel ordered the aide-de-camp and driver to lead the way back to the vehicle. Along the way, Stojkovic had plenty of opportunities for betrayal. Companies of men maneuvered forward, some of them close enough for Swayne to reach out and touch as they went by. He kept his head lowered, and was glad for the dim light of dusk. Anybody who stopped him to ask questions might have to be killed. He did not know how Stojkovic might act if the Marines began killing his men.

When they reached the SUV, they found the rear gate open and the backseats down so they could slide the litter forward.

But when Swayne and Night Runner turned around, they found themselves looking into two sets of angry eyes. The aide-de-camp and nervous driver held automatic pistols on them and the colonel.

Stojkovic spoke harshly, his tone indicating that he wanted to know what the hell was going on. The major answered, speaking with disdain.

"He heard us speaking English," the colonel said, sounding defeated. "And he realized that Markocevik could not have been injured by an explosive because there was no explosion."

The major, apparently agitated at the fate of his general and the treachery of the colonel, shifted his weight from foot to foot.

Stojkovic said, "Perhaps I could have some of my men arrest these two."

"No," said Swayne. "If you say anything, he's liable to start shooting."

The major hollered at them.

"He's telling us to stop talking English," Stojkovic said.

"He's as psychotic as his boss," said Night Runner. "He's trying to get up the nerve to kill us all. I'm going to take him."

Night Runner's hands moved slowly toward the sheath of his sword.

The major shifted his aim to Night Runner's face and barked another order—or was it a threat? Swayne heard a buzz in his ear and spoke up quickly: "No, no." He dropped to his knees, pleading, as if for his life. Only the words did not add up. "Colonel, Night Runner," he wailed. "Get down on your knees and act as if you are praying. Now."

The major looked confused at three men suddenly turned to cowards. The tips of Swayne's folded hands touched the button of his microphone.

"Just the two of them, Henry," Swayne said. "Just the two of them."

TWO OF THEM, hell, thought Friel. He could take out half a dozen before any one of them knew that they had been shot at. But Swayne had spoken. One armor-piercing round of titanium steel was barely on its way toward the head of the major before the second bullet picked up its target, the driver. The rounds, with their video imagers in the projectiles, sped toward the two men.

Friel, the consummate sniper, had already shifted to an alternate firing position. And he was already searching the dim forest through his scope, looking for a third target. Nobody was close by.

The colonel, his forehead rippled with questions, stared at Swayne.

Until two snaps like breaking pencils sounded over his head, and the major and Markocevik's driver morphed into fountains of spewing blood, the impact creating a vacuum inside their heads. The sudden backflow of pressure equalizing expelled their eyeballs.

Night Runner and Swayne were on their feet before the pair hit the ground.

"Into the truck, Colonel. You drive. How about sharing your plan for getting out of here with Markocevik." Swayne touched the button of his microphone. "Henry, I don't know whether to kiss you or court-martial you. Do you want to join up with us, or can you evade the Serbs and do what I told you to do in the first place?"

The colonel interrupted. "I will call off my brigade. They still do not know that Markocevik relieved me of my command. They will do what I tell them."

Swayne nodded, listening both to the colonel and to Friel's smart-aleck reply in his ear: "I'd appreciate it if you wouldn't court-martial me, but I'd appreciate it more if you wouldn't kiss me. I was going to check on the sick, lame, and lazy, Boss. But first I wanted to see if I needed to save your asses. Good thing, huh?"

Swayne snorted in reply.

Friel explained that too many soldiers were running around the woods for him to try to sneak through. "Better I go find the lost sheep and wait to get picked up."

Swayne told him to get going, the tone of his voice expressing his gratitude. Then he listened to Stojkovic's plan and nodded his approval. Finally he felt free to transmit to Zavello, asking him to shut off the bombing. He asked that Zavello send in fighters to clear a path for him and the others to escape with Markocevik from Kosovo. And, of course, he arranged for Henry Friel's clear sailing back to the LZ where Perfect, Nina, the video, and Petr the Kosovar were to be airlifted.

Finally he asked that Stojkovic's combat unit be spared. It was an appeal to Zavello's own code of honor among warriors. Zavello honored it without hesitation. Instead he issued frag orders for bombings along the border where armor units had been massed, trying to cut off Swayne's escape route.

EPILOGUE

NIGHT RUNNER HAD begun to doubt the warrior class of white men until he saw the behavior of the colonel, Swayne, and Zavello. It made him believe that these soldiers could be as civilized as his own people in matters of battle. True to his word and his plan, the colonel drove them to Markocevik's helicopter. The instant he stopped the vehicle, he began acting excited, as if this was a matter of life and death, which it certainly appeared to be once Swayne and Night Runner carried the litter, literally filled with blood and guts, to the helicopter. The aircrew did not even notice Night Runner and Swayne, so transfixed were they at the sight of the apparently mortally wounded Markocevik.

SWAYNE DOUBTED THE wisdom of leaving the country with only half of his Force Recon Team. In flight, a sudden idea occurred to him, and he asked the colonel to divert the helicopter to the landing zone where they were to meet Perfect and pick up Nina and Petr. But when they arrived, they found nothing. Stojkovic ordered the crew to circle the area a while, but when they began receiving ground fire, Swayne decided they had better leave the country and take their precious cargo of Markocevik someplace where he could be put into NATO custody.

Almost immediately after landing, member countries began fighting over control of Markocevik. Swayne realized that his worst fears would come true—that Markocevik would get lost in the diplomatic shuffle and eventually go free. Unless that tape were somehow to materialize. He and Night Runner didn't have time to worry about matters of global importance. Two of their men were still inside Kosovo. They rearmed and refreshed themselves quickly, and boarded a stealth helicopter that flew them toward the border nearest the pickup zone. While they were still in the air, they heard from Friel.

FRIEL HAD DOUBTED that Perfect could have pulled off his part of the mission, and before long he saw that he was right, although it gave him little satisfaction. Perfect's corpse lay on the trail, where Petr and his band of Kosovars had left it. Friel got no satisfaction out of being right. He made his report to Swayne, and together they arranged to meet in an area less than two hundred meters away, where the stealth helicopter could land and retrieve the Marine's body.

Swayne wanted to know if there was anything to report about Petr. When Friel told him his answer, Swayne asked about the babe. After that, there was a long period of silence until Swayne, his voice not quite right, asked about the dog.

Friel opened his mouth to give yet another negative answer, but did not speak. Coming at him through the low brush, his head held low, was a golden retriever. The animal sidled next to Friel, who had never shown

it any particular interest, and forced its square head under Friel's hand.

Friel stroked the dog's head and scratched its neck.
He didn't trust the animal to stay with him, so he took
a grip on its collar and began to work off his belt so he
could use it as a leash. The collar felt too tight, and he
thought he should loosen it. That was when he found
the videotape.

Friel tried to put himself into Perfect's shoes. For
some reason he had thought he might be in danger of
losing the videotape cassette. And, of course, he had
trusted the dog more than himself. So what he had done
made sense. He had pulled the tape out of the cassette,
wrapped it in a loop that fit beneath the dog's collar,
covered it with an elastic bandage, and secured it with
bad-ass duct tape.

Perfect wasn't so perfect after all. But he had done
the right thing. The kid was a hero. Because of him, the
Spartans would be able to accomplish their mission.
Friel took off his own jacket and covered the man's
body, protecting it from the weather and the insects, af-
fording respect to the corpse he never gave to the man.

NINA AWAKENED IN a hospital bed doubting whether she
could continue as a CNN reporter. She had seen enough
death and destruction in her last three times out on as-
signments. And each time, she had flown nearer the sun,
this time nearly getting herself killed. She had her story.
And it was a painful one to tell. The Kosovars were kind
enough to transport her overland to Albania, where she
could be turned over to a NATO unit. They would not
turn over the tape cassette, however. They had their own
purposes for it. And along the way, she saw them line
up a squad of captured Serbs and do to them what the
Serbs had done to Kosovars—and herself. There was no
civility to this thing called war, and she wanted no part
of it again.

• • •

EVENTUALLY FRIEL TURNED over the coil of videotape to the Marine Corps. He would not take his hand off the dog's collar until he could put it directly into Swayne's hands. Swayne would not release it to anybody short of Zavello himself.

Zavello ordered a communications technician to prepare the tape for viewing, and a crowd of battle-hardened Marines watched in horror as the mass murder unfolded.

The tape made its way to the White House. After that, it vanished from public view.

Markocevik never went to trial, but was held and used as leverage to get secret concessions from the Serbs, who preferred to trade a truce for videotaped revelations about the atrocities. Eventually, Markocevik and the tape were sent back to the land where they originated.

Less than a month later, Markocevik was dead, assassinated by terrorists unknown, presumably Kosovars, but more likely his colleagues. Less than three months after that, the former president was arrested and tried for war crimes.

Zavello showed the secret intelligence reports of his death to Swayne the day after the assassination. "You and your team were in the middle of the shit," Zavello growled. "Least we can do is let you know how it turned out."

Swayne wondered how Zavello could know about Markocevik's death so quickly and with such certainty. But he did not say anything.

Zavello handed him a videocassette.

Swayne blinked but held his tongue. He knew what it was. A copy of the murders.

"I thought about dropping it into the hands of the freaking media," Zavello said. "Show what kind of an Administration we have that wouldn't do something about this."

Swayne shrugged.

Zavello said, "It's not the kind of thing a Marine Corps officer does. That kind of shit is for the politicians and the bastards in the media."

Swayne shrugged again. What was he supposed to do with it? He was a Marine Corps officer, too.

Zavello showed him out of his office without answering the question for him, and Swayne knew he'd have to settle accounts with himself.

He visited Nina Chase's apartment, where she was recuperating on medical leave from CNN. He made drinks for them, stiff drinks, and built a fire.

Nina said, "You haven't been yourself tonight." She nodded at the videocassette on his lap. "Is that the one?"

"Yes."

"Are you going to give it to the Senator?"

"No."

"Are you going to give it to me?"

"No."

She raised one eyebrow, forming it into a question mark.

He glanced toward the fireplace. "I'm going to burn it."

"Good," she said. "I couldn't bear to live through that again."

SOMETHING EXPLODED IN THE SKY...

...something metallic, something swirling, something from hell. Four dark beasts filled the southeastern horizon like the lions of the Apocalypse. The reflection of morning light off the sand splayed like blood across their wings...

HOGS: GOING DEEP
by James Ferro

___0-425-16856-5/$5.99

Also Available:

___*Hogs #2: Hog Down*   0-425-17039-X/$5.99

___*Hogs #3: Fort Apache*   0-425-17306-2/$5.99

___*Hogs #4: Snake Eaters* 0-425-17815-3/$5.99